"I can giv
on my m

Her heart pounding, Beth gaped at Clay. What could she say? She needed a ride, but a good-looking guy and a motorcycle brought back disturbing memories like a bad dream. The resemblance to the past scared her. She tried to tell herself she was a grown woman now, a mother, not some silly, lonely teenager with a need to be wanted and loved. But she couldn't shake all the echoes of her troubled history.

"You ready?"

"Okay." The word came out in a squeak, and she hoped he wouldn't guess how nervous the prospect of this ride made her. Should she tell him how much she hated motorcycles?

Books by Merrillee Whren

Love Inspired

The Heart's Homecoming #314
An Unexpected Blessing #352
Love Walked In #378

MERRILLEE WHREN

is the winner of the 2003 Golden Heart Award for best inspirational-romance manuscript presented by Romance Writers of America. In 2004 she made her first sale to Steeple Hill. She is married to her own personal hero, her husband of twenty-nine years, and has two grown daughters. She has lived in Atlanta, Boston, Dallas and Chicago, but now makes her home on one of God's most beautiful creations, an island off the east coast of Florida. When she's not writing or working for her husband's recruiting firm, she spends her free time playing tennis or walking the beach, where she does the plotting for her novels.

Merrillee loves to hear from readers. You can contact her through her Web site at www.merrilleewhren.com.

MERRILLEE WHREN

Love Walked In

Steeple
Hill®

Published by Steeple Hill Books™

STEEPLE HILL BOOKS

Steeple
Hill®

ISBN-13: 978-0-373-87412-5
ISBN-10:   0-373-87412-X

LOVE WALKED IN

www.SteepleHill.com

Printed in U.S.A.

For it is by grace you have been saved, through faith—and this not from yourselves, it is the gift of God—not by works, so that no one can boast.
—*Ephesians* 2:8–9

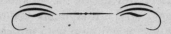

This book is dedicated to the memory of my wonderful parents, George and Gladys Luft, who created a loving family atmosphere and taught me about the love of God when I was a child.

Thanks to my brother George and his wonderful bride, Arleen, for taking me on a tour of Pend Oreille County. And a final thank you to my friend, Marita Norton, for her help with information about the North Pend Oreille Valley Lions Club Excursion Train. Any mistakes are strictly mine.

Chapter One

❦

The roar of a motorcycle shattered the quiet of the warm August afternoon. A Harley cruised to a stop behind the red SUV parked at the curb. Rider and machine appeared as one, black-and-silver power. Beth Carlson halted mid-step on the wooden porch that wrapped around the front and side of the white two-story house—her new home. Her heart pounding, she clutched the large cardboard box in her arms.

Quiet returned as the rider cut the motor. Dismounting, he flipped back the visor of his silver helmet like a knight returning victorious from battle. While he strode up the walk, he took off the helmet and tucked it under one arm. His black T-shirt, faded black jeans and long dark hair, pulled back in a ponytail, gave him a rugged, rebellious look.

Beth's mouth went dry. Her heart raced as she stared at the stranger. Meeting new people always made her nervous. Blinking, she tried to focus her attention somewhere else, but his approach captured her gaze like the fly caught in the spiderweb hanging in the corner of the porch. When he looked her way, a sense of déjà vu swept over her. Yet there was nothing familiar about his handsome face.

Hoping to push aside her anxiety, Beth opened the screen door and set the box down just over the threshold. Then she turned to Kim Petit, the friend who was helping her move. "Who's that?"

"Clay Reynolds. I told you about him."

"You mean the guy who moved into the upstairs apartment?" Beth willed her heart to quit hammering against her rib cage.

"Yeah. Come on. I'll introduce you, but first you've got to close your mouth and quit drooling," Kim kidded.

Clamping her mouth shut, Beth berated herself for giving Kim the wrong idea. She let the screen door bang shut and reluctantly followed Kim to the porch steps. Nothing about this man impressed Beth. Everything about him made her want to run the other way. Motorcycles and men who rode them only reminded her of a past she didn't want to think about.

"Hey, Clay," Kim called. "I want you to meet Beth Carlson."

He took the two steps leading to the porch in one stride. His expression exuded confidence. He smiled, and his gray eyes twinkled as he extended his hand. "Hi, Beth. I hear we're going to be neighbors."

"I guess so." Pushing up her glasses, she pasted a smile onto her face. As his large hand firmly gripped hers, shivers raced down her spine. Not shivers of excitement but of unease. The smooth sound of his deep voice made her apprehensive. This man and his motor-cycle dredged up memories of her troubled teenage years. Memories she had tried to bury.

"You've got great timing, Clay," Kim said, taking his arm.

"Is that right?" He gave Kim a curious glance before letting his attention settle on Beth.

Kim nudged him with an elbow. "We need your help moving Beth's stuff."

"Let me head up to my apartment first. Then I'll be right back to help."

Beth watched him disappear around the corner of the porch. When she was sure he was out of earshot, she looked at Kim. "He works for Jillian Lawson? He doesn't look like the corporate type."

Kim nodded. "Yeah. Surprised me when Jillian introduced us at church. He's a lawyer and works as a consultant. Mostly with nonprofit organizations. While she's on maternity leave, he's here to oversee her charitable foundation. Good-looking guy, isn't he?"

Beth shrugged. "If you like that type."

"What's not to like?"

"He's just not my type." Beth shoved at her glasses again. "Besides, all the good-looking guys I've met go for tall, skinny, bleached blondes." Beth flipped her hair with one hand. "Not dishwater blondes with a few extra pounds on the hips."

Kim shook her head. "Beth, you underestimate yourself."

"It doesn't matter. I'm not interested."

"You could've fooled me. I saw the way you looked at him."

Beth gazed across the yard at the motorcycle. Its chrome gleamed in the sunshine filtering through the trees that lined the street. She couldn't go into the reasons she had no interest in her new neighbor. Bringing up the past would only create a gulf between her and Kim.

Beth didn't want that. When she moved to this little town in eastern Washington State a couple of years ago, Kim had befriended Beth. That friendship meant more to her than just about anything except her son, Max. The fact that Kim didn't pry was a wonderful bonus to her friendship.

Beth tried to smile. "My *look* had nothing to do with *his* looks. The noise startled me, and I don't like motorcycles."

"If you say so." Kim hopped down from the porch and headed for the SUV. "Let's carry in some more boxes."

"Sure." Beth started down the steps, too, but footfalls on the porch captured her attention. As Clay appeared from around the corner, her stomach lurched. Why did she react so much to this guy? Just because he was a handsome man? She hated her body's betrayal.

Grinning, he gave her a salute. "Reporting for duty. What do you want me to do?"

Beth's mind went blank. His presence had her completely discombobulated. And it wasn't just the fact that he was good-looking. Ever since she could remember, meeting new people had made her uneasy. Although she had moved several times as a child, she had never overcome the inability to make friends with ease. And now even this simple move across town to less cramped quarters for her and her teenage son brought with it the uncomfortable task of meeting someone new.

"Help us bring in these boxes from the back of my SUV," Kim answered before Beth could open her mouth.

"Where's that husband of yours?" Clay asked Kim as Beth joined her on the front walk.

"Brian's with Sam and Max. They're using Sam's truck to move Beth's furniture. They'll be here soon."

"You mean Sam isn't hovering over Jillian? I thought he wouldn't let her out of his sight with the baby due so soon. Less than a month now, isn't it?"

Nodding, Kim laughed and opened the back of the SUV. "Jillian's spending the afternoon with her parents. That's the only way my brother would leave her. Sam is driving everyone nuts, including his wife. I'll be glad when my nephew is born."

Beth watched Kim with envy as Clay picked up a box and handed it to her. Not because Beth wished for his attention, but because Kim had such a natural way with people. She could strike up a conversation with anyone about anything at any time. Beth wished for that ability.

Giving herself a mental shake, Beth told herself that the world needed all kinds of people. Quiet people counted, too. Not everyone could be the life of the party.

"Who's Max?" Clay balanced two boxes in his arms.

"My son." Beth joined the duo at the back of the SUV. "He'll be a sophomore in high school this year."

"You have a son in high school?" Clay's brow wrinkled. "You look too young to have a son that age."

"Well, I do." Shrugging, Beth grabbed a box. She didn't want to explain why, at thirty-one, she had a fifteen-year-old son.

Before anyone could say another word, a horn

honked. Beth looked up. A shiny blue-and-silver pickup truck loaded with furniture pulled up beside Kim's SUV.

Brian Petit, Kim's husband, leaned out the passenger window. "Hey, Beth, where should we park?"

She moved to the curb and pointed. "In front of Kim's SUV." After they parked, he and Sam Lawson emerged from the truck. Beth stepped into the street. "Where's Max?"

Brian shrugged. "Isn't he here?"

"I thought he was meeting you to help you load the furniture after school. He's had plenty of time to get there." Beth pushed at her glasses again. "Do you suppose football practice ran long today?"

"That's probably it. The coaches are pushing them hard. The first game's only a couple of weeks away," Brian said.

"You're probably right." Beth tried to convince herself of that scenario. Max was a good kid. She shouldn't worry.

Clay soon joined Brian and Sam as they moved beds, chests and a big oak table into the house while Beth and Kim finished bringing in the boxes. When Beth brought in the last carton, Brian stood in the doorway to her bedroom just off the living room to the right.

"Hey, Beth, come here and tell us if this is how you want your furniture arranged." Brian stepped aside.

Perusing the room, Beth took in the battered oak chest and dresser. Her beloved stuff looked a bit dingy in the bright light shining through the window that looked out onto the front porch. But it was sturdy and serviceable, and she was grateful to have it. She glanced at Brian. "I'd like the chest in that corner by the window. Everything else can stay where it is."

"How about Max's room?" Sam poked his head around the doorframe.

"I'm going to let him do what he wants in there. It's the first time he's had a room that big. So put his stuff anywhere, and he can arrange it later," Beth replied.

Clay picked up a framed picture from a half-opened box sitting on the floor. "Is this Max?"

Beth stepped closer to look. Clay handed her the photo. Setting it on her dresser, she stared at the image of her son with his dark hair and eyes so different from her light hair and blue eyes. She loved Max more than words could express. Despite the heartache of the past, she was glad to have Max. Her son, who now stood a couple of inches taller than six feet, was an attractive young man. Sometimes she worried that he was too handsome for his own good. Like his father. Like her new neighbor.

"Yeah, that's Max, but he's grown nearly a foot since that picture was taken. I could hardly keep him in clothes last year."

"So he's on the football team?" Clay asked as he helped Brian move the chest.

Beth grimaced. "Yeah. I'm not real excited about that. The game's so rough. Makes me cringe when I think about it."

Clay looked back at Beth. "What position does he play?"

"Wide receiver. Whatever that means." Beth shrugged.

Clay chuckled. "Sounds like you need someone to fill you in on the finer points of the game."

"Are you volunteering?" Kim came to stand next to Clay.

"Sure." Clay grinned. "I played wide receiver myself when I was in high school."

"Come on, guys." Brian stepped into the room. "No time for football instructions now. We've got more furniture to deliver. One more trip, and that should be it."

"Do you need help?" Clay called after Brian.

Stopping, Brian shook his head. "No, you can help when we get back. For now, you can give Beth a hand unpacking." Brian turned to Beth. "Right, Beth?"

Swallowing hard, Beth looked from Brian to Clay and back to Brian. Why was Kim's husband micromanaging this move? Maybe he was only trying to be helpful, but now she was trapped into spending time alone with a dangerously attractive stranger. She glanced at Clay. "I…Kim's going to help me unpack. So you don't have to."

"Sorry, Beth." Kim shook her head. "Sam asked me to pick up Jillian and some take-out fried chicken from the Pinecrest Café for everyone. We'll eat here after they bring the second load of furniture. Okay?"

"Okay." Beth forced herself to smile. Now *everyone* was micromanaging her move. Or maybe just maneuvering her into spending time alone with Clay. She gave herself a mental shake for being paranoid.

"Then everything's settled." Kim gave Beth a wink as she exited the room with her husband.

Beth stood there surrounded by boxes, and watched everyone leave. Everyone except Clay. Maybe she wasn't being paranoid after all.

After the others left, Clay followed Beth around, waiting to be useful. Her light hair swished around her shoulders as she picked up a box and carried it into her bedroom. She never looked his way. Without saying a word, she pushed at her brown horn-rimmed glasses before she knelt to open a box filled with books.

Finally she looked up at him with a tentative smile. "You don't really have to help. You kinda got pushed into it." She let her gaze fall to a book she lifted from the box. "I won't be offended if you want to leave."

In two strides Clay closed the distance between them. He hunkered down next to her. "I don't mind helping. I can even give you those lessons about football. You should know what's happening when you watch your son play. Besides, we're going to be neighbors."

"That's very kind of you." She raised her eyes to meet his.

The bluest eyes Clay had ever seen stared back at him. His heart did an odd little tap dance. How had he not noticed those eyes before? He had the insane urge to take off her glasses and get a better look at eyes bluer than the cloudless sky outside.

Shaking away the thought, he stood. "What do you want me to do?"

She gave him that little smile again as she dragged the box over to a bookcase sitting against one wall. "See if you can find the other box of books. I think it's in the living room."

As he headed into the living room, he had the distinct impression that pretty Beth Carlson felt uncomfortable in his presence. Maybe she was naturally shy and being alone with a stranger made her nervous. With the image of her brilliant blue eyes fixed in his brain, he scanned the room for a box of books. He spotted a carton with bold black lettering on one side: **Books.** He picked it up and headed for the bedroom.

When he entered the room, she turned toward him. "Oh, good. You found them. Thanks."

"Yep." With a thud, he set the box on the floor next to the bookcase. "Now what do you want me to do?" Those big blue eyes looked back at him, and his heart did that strange little tap dance again.

"You can put the books on the shelves while I do this other stuff."

"Sure." He settled on the floor beside the bookshelf. What did these books say about their owner? *The Poetry of Robert Frost, An Anthology of Children's Literature, The Way Things Work,* and a battered Bible were the first four books he pulled from the box. An interesting mix. Both poetic and child-friendly. "Do you want your Bible in the bookcase?"

She turned to look at him. "Yes, that's fine. It's not my Bible. It was my great-aunt's. I just keep it for sentimental value. I don't actually read it."

"I have a Bible like that, too. It belonged to my grandfather." Clay put the books on a shelf. "Do you attend the same church as the Petits and Lawsons?"

"No, I don't go to church."

Clay didn't know what to say. "Oh…I thought since you were such a good friend of Kim's that you probably went to the same church."

Beth smiled shyly. "It's not like she hasn't tried to get me to attend."

"And why hasn't she succeeded?"

"Because I don't see the need for church. My dad's a preacher, so I've heard enough sermons to last me a lifetime." As if to signal an end to the topic, Beth turned away and busied herself emptying boxes on the other side of the room.

Stunned by her pronouncement, Clay grabbed a few more books and put them away. Wow! A preacher's kid who had no use for church. Usually he didn't have trouble finding something to talk about, but he was at a loss for words. Rather than saying the wrong thing, he put the books away in silence.

When he finished, he looked up to find Beth taking bubble wrap from a ballerina figurine. She tossed the bubble wrap into the empty box near her feet. Tinkling musical notes danced through the air as she gently placed the figurine on her dresser.

He stood. "A music box?"

Turning, she nodded. The look on her face made him think she had almost forgotten he was there. She gave the ballerina a gentle twist. While a lilting tune filled the room, the porcelain ballerina spun gracefully on her stand. "It was my great-aunt's. In fact, almost everything in this room once belonged to her."

Clay took in the crocheted doilies that graced the nightstand and dresser. They reminded him of his grandmother's house. Decor from a bygone era. "Did your great-aunt make the doilies?"

"Yes, she loved to crochet. She tried to teach me how, but I was all thumbs." Beth smiled again, but this time her eyes lit up, and the smile spread to her whole face. Just as quickly, the smile disappeared. "I miss her. She died two years ago after a long illness."

"I'm sorry for your loss," Clay replied, feeling his response to be strangely inadequate.

"Thanks. I have lots of good memories of Aunt Violet."

"Did she live here in Pinecrest?"

"No, but she had a friend who used to. After my aunt died, that friend put me in touch with her daughter, who still lives here. She's the principal of the elementary school. She helped me get my job. That's what brought me to Pinecrest."

"So you're a teacher?"

"No, a teacher's aide. Kindergarten." Beth dropped her gaze. "I want to be a teacher. I take night and weekend classes in Spokane. The teacher I'm an aide for is retiring next year, so I'm hoping to get that job."

"Your job and classes must keep you busy."

"They do, but I have a few days to get settled here before teachers and aides report next week."

"Do you like living in Pinecrest?"

Smiling, she nodded. "I do. It's home to me now."

"Small-town life isn't for me. I prefer the big city. Thankfully I'm only here for a few months to look after Jillian's foundation while she's out on leave."

"And how do you know Jillian?" Beth picked up a couple of empty boxes.

"I did all the legal work when she set up her foundation. Nonprofit organizations are my specialty."

Beth headed for the door. "Then you must know a lot about it."

"I do, and I'm also glad to help out a friend whose foundation helps a lot of worthy causes, like the assisted living center she plans to build here in Pinecrest." Clay grabbed the empty box sitting near his feet and followed Beth.

"And the children's home that Sam has started," Beth added.

As they stepped into the living room, Kim dashed in through the front door. "Jillian's gone into labor!" Kim blurted and paused to catch her breath. "When I stopped to pick her up, she had already called Sam. They're headed to the hospital. Brian will be here in a minute with Sam's truck and your furniture. Then we're headed that way. Sorry about not finishing up here, but maybe Clay and Max can do that."

"No problem." Clay glanced out the front door as Brian emerged from Sam's truck and headed for the SUV.

Dropping the boxes, Beth rushed to Kim's side and gave her a hug. "Don't worry about me and my stuff. Tell Jillian and Sam I'm thinking of them. Call me about the baby as soon as you can. Okay?"

"Sure," Kim replied.

Stepping onto the front porch, Beth called after Kim as she sprinted down the front walk. "Did Max ever show up?"

"No," Kim yelled. "We never saw him."

Beth grabbed hold of one of the porch supports and held so tightly that her knuckles turned white. Leaning her head against the support, she let out a shaky breath.

"Are you okay?" Clay joined her on the front porch.

Turning, she looked at him. Even her horn-rimmed glasses didn't hide the tears welling in her eyes. "I—I'm not sure." She pushed at her glasses and glanced at her watch. "I'm worried. Max knew we were moving today. Even if practice ran long, he should've been here by now."

"Can you reach him on a cell phone?"

Beth shook her head. "No, he doesn't have one."

"Do you need to look for him?"

She nodded. "Yes, though I can't imagine where he would be."

"You go. I'll stay here and keep an eye on Sam's truck and unload some of your stuff."

She glanced at her watch again. "Thanks. I'll check the high school. It isn't far. I shouldn't be long."

Clay followed her into the kitchen. "Take your time. While you're gone, I can empty the boxes in here and set the stuff on the counters for you to put away later."

"That would be great. Thanks." She grabbed her purse from the kitchen counter and raced out the door.

Through the kitchen window Clay watched her run down the walk toward the freestanding garage by the alley. His heart did that funny little skip. What was happening to him? There was something about this shy, pretty woman with the sparkling blue eyes that created strange sensations in his chest. He shook his head, trying to erase the image of those eyes filled with tears. He reminded himself that she wasn't his type, especially because she didn't seem to care about church or, likely, God.

When she was out of sight, he opened a box and removed its contents. Setting a stack of plates on the counter, he wondered how he was going to deal with his new neighbor. Could he be a witness for the Lord without making her angry? Maybe the easiest thing to do was just help her out when she needed it. Like now. But his unexpected attraction to her sent up warning signals in his mind. As he emptied the first box, the back door slammed. He spun around.

Beth stomped across the room and slapped her purse onto the round oak table in the middle of the kitchen.

Her eyes flashed bright blue with fury. "My car just died. Now what do I do?"

"Hey, I know a little about cars. Maybe it's something simple. You want me to take a look?"

She shrugged. "It couldn't hurt."

Clay followed her out through the backyard. As they turned into the alley, he saw an old gray sedan with a rusted fender stalled halfway between the garage and the street at the other end of the alley.

When they reached the car, he said, "Pop the hood."

She opened the car door, tossed her purse in and slid behind the wheel.

When Clay heard the click that released the hood, he opened it. "Okay, give it a try."

Nothing happened. She poked her head out the window. "It doesn't start. Do I have a dead battery?"

"Probably, but I think your real problem is your alternator. When it goes bad, it drains the battery, too."

"Now what?" She pushed at her glasses.

"Well, first we need to get your car out of the alley."

"And how do you propose to do that when it won't start?"

"Push it."

"Push it?"

"Yeah, put it in Neutral, and I'll push. Once it's moving, you can steer. I should be able to push it out to the street. You pull it next to the curb."

"This will work?" She stared at him with a frown.

He couldn't help smiling. "Sure. You've never had to do this with a car before?"

She shook her head. "Never."

"Well, you get to experience something new today,"

he said, thinking he'd experienced something new himself. Being attracted to a woman he shouldn't be attracted to. How was he going to avoid her when she lived right downstairs? How could he ignore her when she needed his help?

"Okay, I hope this works. What exactly do I do?"

Clay placed his hands on the car. "I'll count to three, then push."

"I'm ready."

"Here we go. One, two, three." He pushed.

The clunky car didn't budge.

"Now what?" Beth's eyebrows knit together.

"I'll give it another try." Clay glanced at her. "Ready?"

"Okay."

"One, two, three."

The car started moving.

"All right," Beth cried with a big grin covering her face.

"Don't sit there grinning. Steer."

"Oh…oh, yeah."

The car moved with ease down the alley and into the street. "Turn the wheel," Clay yelled. He breathed a sigh of relief when she managed to get the car reasonably close to the curb. "Okay, stop. We've got it."

After she braked the car to a halt, Beth hopped out and looked at Clay. "Well, we got the car out of the alley, but that still doesn't solve my transportation problem."

"What about Sam's truck?"

"Besides the fact that it's filled with furniture, I don't have the key."

Clay rubbed the back of his neck as he kicked at a pebble lying in the street. "That leaves one option. I can give you a ride on my bike."

Her big blue eyes stared at him from behind her glasses. The expression on her face suggested that she thought he had just asked her to take a ride with a stunt driver.

Chapter Two

Her heart pounding, Beth gaped at Clay. What could she say? She needed a ride, but a good-looking guy and a motorcycle brought back disturbing memories like a bad dream. The resemblance to the past scared her. Not to mention the very real dangers of riding a motorcycle. She tried to tell herself she was a grown woman now, not some silly, lonely teenager with a need to be wanted and loved. But she couldn't shake all the echoes of her troubled history.

"You ready?" He stared at her.

"Okay." The word came out in a squeak, and she hoped he wouldn't guess how nervous the prospect of this ride made her. Should she tell him how much she hated motorcycles? Why should he care? Besides, she didn't have a choice. Finding Max was more important than her problems from the past. Taking a deep breath, she squared her shoulders and followed Clay through the alley to the house.

When they reached the porch, he turned. "Wait here. I've got to get my helmet."

Taking the steps two at a time, he climbed the stairs to his apartment. She closed her eyes and tried to block out his image. He was being too nice. Just like Scott Harkin, Max's dad. At fifteen she'd been bowled over by Scott's charm and flattered beyond reason that a good-looking guy with lots of money would pay attention to her. But he hadn't cared about her. He just wanted to win a bet that he could make it with the preacher's daughter. The truth pierced her soul even now.

Beth shook away the painful memories. She reminded herself again that she wasn't a kid anymore. She could handle this guy. She wouldn't be drawn in by his kind deeds or compliments. She knew his type. They thought they had an infallible way with women just because they were handsome. Walking to the other end of the porch, she wished she had some other way to find Max.

Hearing footsteps, she turned. Clay's muscular form and ponytail, silhouetted against the late afternoon sun, captivated and frightened her at the same time. Though entranced, she forced herself to look away.

When he reached her side, he handed her a helmet. "One for you. Ready?"

"Y-yes," she replied breathlessly. Her palms sweating, she balanced the helmet in her hands. "Do you always keep an extra one with you?"

Grinning, he put on his helmet. "Yeah. For occasions like this when I can take a pretty woman for a ride."

His words brought back the past like a dagger to the heart. Making no comment, she refused to fall for his flattery. She'd done that once in her life. Never again. His statement confirmed her opinion that he was like all the other attractive men she'd known. They knew how to feed a girl a line. She would wager anything that he didn't really believe she was pretty.

Mounting the bike, he gave her a smile that made her shiver with apprehension. "Hop on."

Pushing aside the emotions that bombarded her, she forced herself to return his smile and climbed aboard. Settling on the leather seat, she tried to ignore the closeness of his body. His nearness had her senses on overload.

Get a grip. "Do you know where the high school is?"

"Sure. Sam and Jillian took me on a tour of the town last Sunday after church. It's out near the highway, right?"

"Yeah."

"Okay. Put your arms around my waist, keep your head over my shoulder and align your body with mine," he instructed as the engine roared to life. "Hang on," he shouted over the noise.

The motorcycle sped away from the curb and down the shady, tree-lined street. Beth wrapped her arms around his lean torso. She tried to concentrate on finding Max. This was for him. The wind whipped strands of hair around her shoulders and ruffled the sleeves of her shirt, but Clay's body shielded the rest of her. She didn't know whether the pounding of her pulse was due to the exhilarating ride or the feel of Clay's hard-muscled frame in her arms. Either way, she tried to steel herself against feeling anything. She let a silent mantra course through her mind: *This is for Max. This is for Max.*

Clay cruised through the center of town. The post office, gas station, drugstore and grocery were a blur as they whizzed by. In the distance Beth spied the high school and hoped Max would be there.

When Clay drove into the empty parking lot near the

football field, Beth's heart sank. Now what? She didn't voice the words aloud. She had repeated that phrase too many times today.

Clay brought the motorcycle to a stop and flipped up the visor on his helmet. He turned. "No one's here. What do you want to do?"

She wanted to cry, but she couldn't do that. Not in front of a man she barely knew. She tried to think, but worry froze her thoughts. She shrugged and blinked back tears. Pressing her lips together, she fought the sob that welled up in her chest.

Before she could come up with an answer, Clay asked, "Where do the high school kids usually hang out?"

Beth stared at Clay. She didn't have a clue. Max didn't "hang out." He always came home. She racked her brain for an answer. "Maybe the Dairy Dream on the other side of town?"

"You wanna go there?"

"I suppose."

As they sped away, Beth hoped her guess was a good one. But why would Max go to the Dairy Dream when he knew she needed him to help with the move? Not showing up was so unlike him. If he was going to be late, he always called. Maybe he had been hurt at football practice and was on the way to the hospital. And no one could get in touch with her because she'd been out messing with her stalled car and now on a wild-goose chase through town. She bemoaned the prohibitive cost of cell phones and tried to rein in her runaway imagination as they negotiated the turn onto the street where the Dairy Dream was located.

The giant vanilla ice-cream cone sitting atop the

Dairy Dream loomed in the distance. Several cars were parked in front. A group of people sat at a picnic table at the back of the building. She strained to see if one of them was Max. When they drew closer, she recognized the green knit shirt he had worn when he left the house for football practice.

The smell of hamburgers and fries wafted their way as they pulled into the parking area just off the street. Relief washed over her at the same time that anger welled up inside her. Why would Max do this?

She thought she knew why when she saw the cute little redheaded girl who gazed up at him with undisguised adoration. Beth gritted her teeth as the bike came to a stop.

With the motor still idling, Clay removed his helmet and nodded toward the picnic table. "Is that Max over there?"

"Yes, and I'm going to give him a piece of my mind." She scrambled off the bike and in a swift motion took off the helmet and shoved it at Clay as he cut the motor.

He grabbed hold of her arm. "Beth, wait."

"What for?" She turned and glared at him.

"I know you're upset with Max, but marching over there and embarrassing him in front of his friends won't help."

"And what makes you such an expert in dealing with teenagers?"

Getting off the motorcycle, he grinned. "It hasn't been that long since I was in high school, and I remember what it was like. Think back to your own teen years."

That's the last thing she wanted to do. She'd had enough reminders this afternoon. The only thing she wanted to do with her teen years was forget them. Bury them more and more until she couldn't remember them. She jerked her arm out of his grasp. "Mind your own business, and let me deal with my son."

"Okay, if that's what you want." His grin faded.

"It is." She spit out the words and turned toward the picnic table.

As she took a step, she glanced at the group gathered there. Max had no idea she was even here. He only had eyes for the sweet young thing sitting next to him. He said something, and the girl laughed. Beth swallowed a lump in her throat. Max was growing up too fast. He wasn't her little boy anymore.

Releasing a heavy sigh, she turned back and retraced her steps while she kept her eyes trained on the ground. She didn't want to see the look in Clay's eyes. When she reached the bike, she forced herself to look up. His somber expression greeted her.

She stopped in front of him. "I'm sorry. You were right. I almost made a huge mistake."

A lopsided smile crept across his face. "Thanks. I accept your apology. Would you like me to go over there and introduce myself? Tell Max you'd like to see him?"

Beth nodded. "I think that would be okay. I'll wait here."

Clay walked away, and she watched his easy gait as he approached the teenagers. When Clay reached the group, Max glanced up. Clay stepped closer and extended his hand across the table to Max. Smiling, he stood and appeared to be introducing Clay to the entire group. While she watched, she realized her son hadn't inherited her introverted tendencies. That made her happy.

After the introductions, Clay said something else and nodded in her direction. Max's head swung toward her, and even from a distance she recognized an expression of regret. She waved, and he immediately stood, stepped over the bench of the picnic table and jogged toward her. Clay followed close behind.

"Hey, Mom, I'm really sorry. After practice the guys invited me out, and I just forgot." Apprehension painted his face.

"Yes, I guess you did," Beth replied in the calmest voice she could muster.

"Don't be angry."

"I'm disappointed."

Max hung his head. "I'm sorry."

"Well, what do you plan to do about it?"

"I'll come home right now."

"How?"

"The guys will give me a ride." Max cast a look in the direction of his friends.

"Okay, I'll meet you at home." Beth grabbed the helmet that hung from the handlebars.

"Sure, Mom."

"Max," Clay said, stepping beside Beth, "why don't you ask your friends if they'd help move the furniture? And then, if it's okay with your mom, we could order pizza for everyone. Of course, they'd have to check with their parents, too. We don't want any more upset parents."

Max looked at Beth. "Is that okay with you, Mom?"

"Yeah. Now get going."

Max jogged back to his friends and started talking to them. Then one of the boys pulled a cell phone from his pocket and punched in a number. Soon he and several others were calling their parents. In a few minutes Max gave them the thumbs-up sign and joined his friends as they headed to one of the parked cars.

Beth turned to Clay. "Thanks. You were really a life-saver for me today. I don't know how I can ever repay you."

"No payment expected. Just being neighborly." He climbed aboard the bike. "Let's get back before the kids do."

While Clay maneuvered the motorcycle across town, Beth tried not to think about this man whose good looks and kindness made her wish for a moment that she were one of those tall, willowy blondes who attracted men like him. She didn't want to think about it. But now that her worries regarding Max were over, there was nothing else to occupy her mind. Having Clay Reynolds for a neighbor was going to test her resolve not to let down her defenses.

Maybe Clay wasn't like Max's dad, but that didn't change the fact that she wasn't his type. Besides being a plain Jane, she wasn't interested in God or church, and he wasn't a stay-around guy. He was here in Pinecrest for a few months only, and then he'd be gone. She'd had enough of people in her life leaving. She didn't need any more.

When they reached the house, Clay pulled the bike to a stop at the curb and removed his helmet. "Enjoy the ride?"

Beth nodded, unable to speak.

"I like having your arms around me, but if we're going to finish moving you in, you've got to let go."

"Sorry." Blushing, Beth dropped her arms from his waist and alighted from the motorcycle. She took off the helmet and handed it to him.

"Don't be sorry. I was enjoying it." He swung his leg over the seat and faced her, a wry smile curving his lips. "We can move the furniture as soon as I put away these helmets. It's too easy for someone to take them if I leave them on my bike."

As she watched him jog toward the house, she thought she would die of embarrassment. The man had her acting like a silly schoolgirl. Oh, well, didn't handsome guys expect women to fall all over themselves when they were around guys like him? He was probably used to it. Her reaction meant nothing to him.

After Clay came downstairs, he walked along the porch to the front of the house. He noticed Beth standing at the back of Sam's truck as she fumbled with the rope tied around the furniture. Clay stopped at the front steps. Even though she had accepted his help, he wasn't sure she was completely comfortable around him. He didn't know what to make of her except that she adored her son. That much was obvious.

As Clay studied her, he wondered about Max's father. Was Beth a widow? Divorced? She hadn't said, and he didn't feel right about asking. Maybe that was something he would learn in time, but at this point he would be unwise to barrage her with such personal questions.

Then there was the matter of the unexpected effect she had on him. Nothing felt normal about this situation. He barely knew the woman, and yet he already had this protective feeling toward her. He had to chalk it up to her devotion to her fatherless son. He still couldn't believe Beth was old enough to have a son Max's age. She didn't look any older than Jillian, who was the same age as he was. Maybe if he avoided looking into those brilliant blue eyes, the pounding sensation in his chest would go away.

While he stood there thinking of the reasons he shouldn't get involved in Beth's life, a dark blue Jeep Cherokee came to a stop behind his bike. Max and his friends spilled from the vehicle. While the teenagers approached Beth, Clay watched, not wanting to intrude.

Max sauntered toward Beth. "Hey, Mom, I want you to meet Alex and Ryan. They're on the team with me." Max smiled at the redheaded girl and her friend. "And this is Brittany and Lisa. They're on the cheerleading squad."

"Hi. I'm glad to meet you." Beth smiled that familiar little smile that gently curved her full lips. Even meeting these teenagers, she seemed shy.

But she hadn't seemed shy when she told Clay he didn't have any business telling her how to deal with her son. Clay grudgingly admired her fierce maternal protectiveness.

Max took the rope from his mom. "Here, let me have that. Looks like you need some help, short stuff."

"Watch it, mister. You may be close to a foot taller than me, but I *am* your mother." Beth tried to put on a stern expression, but a smile escaped, lighting up her face.

Laughing, Max untied the rope. "You gotta learn to take a little teasing, Mom."

"Maybe. As long as you work on not being so forgetful." She raised her eyebrows. "What do you think?"

"You got me there." He put an arm around her shoulders. "But you gotta admit, you're getting shorter every day."

She laughed. "Let's get to work."

Enjoying the exchange between mother and son, Clay hopped off the porch. He made his way across the yard and joined the group. "Now that you have the ropes untied, the guys can bring in the furniture, and you ladies can unpack boxes. Okay, Beth?"

Beth looked his way. The expression on her face made him realize she had forgotten he was there again. Just as she had earlier today. Somehow that knowledge disturbed him. He didn't want to be forgettable. Why was this woman tying his mind into knots?

"Oh…yeah…sure, we can do that." She glanced from him to the girls. "Okay with you, kids?"

"Yeah," the girls chorused.

While Beth, Brittany and Lisa headed for the house, Clay and the boys unloaded a couch and love seat. Clay surmised that this furniture had also belonged to Beth's great-aunt. He had seen similar furniture in his grandmother's house when he was a kid. The gold cut velour upholstery had been popular over twenty years ago. Despite its age, other than the slightly faded fabric, the furniture was in excellent condition.

The four guys made quick work of moving the living-room furniture into the house. Beth gave orders as to where the various pieces should go while she helped the girls unpack boxes in the dining room, a large open space situated between the living room and kitchen.

Dark oak woodwork ran throughout the house. Built-in curio cabinets about four feet tall with round wooden columns that reached to the ceiling separated the living and dining areas. Beth's bedroom was located off the living room, while Max's bedroom came off the dining room. Even though the house was old, new beige carpeting in the living room and bedrooms and shiny new vinyl flooring in the kitchen gave the place that new construction smell. His apartment was similar but furnished.

"Okay, guys, one last piece," Clay said as he headed out the door.

"Yeah, but this one's going to test some muscles." Max strode down the front walk with Clay.

"I was looking at that monster desk. What's it made of? And how are we going to carry it?" Ryan asked.

"It's solid oak. And yeah, it's heavy." Max hopped up onto the bed of the pickup. "You guys ready for this beast?"

"It would help if we took out the drawers." Clay joined Max.

"Good idea." Max pulled out a drawer and handed it to Ryan, then pulled out another one and gave it to Alex.

After Clay and the boys finished taking the drawers out and putting them in the house, they maneuvered the desk out of the truck and carried it across the lawn. Once on the porch, they set it down, breathing heavily.

"Do you think we can get it through here?" Clay eyed the front door.

Max stepped back and looked. "They got it out of our old place. It should fit."

"I'm wondering how Sam and Brian managed this baby by themselves." Clay eyed Max and wondered whether encouraging Beth to go easy on him in front of his friends had been a good idea. She had expected him to help move their furniture, and maybe she had been right. Clay didn't know much about how to deal with a teenage son. What if Max figured he could get away with this kind of stuff all of the time now? Shaking away the worries, Clay added, "If we take these doors off the hinges, we'll be able to get it through. You got a hammer and screwdriver around here?"

"My mom's got a tool kit." Hurrying into the house, Max let the screen door slam behind him.

Clay followed. Max disappeared into the kitchen. Beth looked up from the box she was emptying. "Where's he going so fast?"

"To get your tool kit," Clay replied. "How's it going in here?"

"Okay. I really appreciate your help. You didn't have to do this."

"I already told you I don't mind." How many times would he have to tell her? "We're getting ready to move that desk in. Where do you want it?"

Beth rose and walked across the room. She stood in the corner next to the big window that overlooked the side porch. "Right here. I'll have to get these boxes out of the way."

"Ms. Carlson, we'll help you." Brittany stood and brushed her red hair behind one ear.

"Thanks, Brittany."

As they moved boxes to the other side of the room, music sounded faintly. Beth reached into one of the cartons. That little smile appeared again when she unwrapped an ornately carved porcelain birdhouse. A lilting tune floated through the air as she carried it into the living room, opened a curio-cabinet door and gently set it inside.

"Another music box?" Clay stepped closer to her.

She nodded. "My great-aunt's collection. These curio cabinets are a perfect place to display them. Unfortunately, my favorite one, a carousel, broke in our original move to Pinecrest."

"That's too bad." Clay turned away, trying not to let those eyes get to him again.

At that moment Max returned with a red plastic case. He opened it up, revealing a hammer, a couple of screwdrivers and other basic tools. "Will these work?"

"Yep." Clay took the case and headed for the door.

Once they had the doors off, they managed to squeeze the desk into the house and place it where Beth had indicated. While Alex and Ryan put the drawers into the desk, Max helped Clay put the doors back on. When that project was complete, Clay surveyed the house. Beth had filled the curio cabinets with music boxes of every shape and size. Animals, a wishing well, a flower cart, a piano and a dozen different water globes.

With her arms crossed, she stood in front of the cabinets. "I wish my great-aunt could see her collection in these beautiful cabinets."

She paused for a moment as if she were going to say something else, but instead, she looked at her watch, then at him. "I think we should order that pizza."

After finding out what toppings everyone wanted, Clay placed the order at a local pizza parlor that the kids recommended. While they waited for the pies, they finished emptying the cartons, and Beth got a good start on putting away her kitchenware. When the doorbell rang, she grabbed her purse and went to the front door.

Clay wanted to pay—the wages of a teacher's aide probably didn't go far—but he feared embarrassing her if he insisted. Somehow he would have to figure out a way to help her. After all, the pizza had been his idea.

Besides, now she had car repairs to deal with. He could get someone from the church who was good with cars. But would Beth accept help from him or the church when she didn't have any use for God?

Chapter Three

Beth fumbled in her purse and hoped she had enough cash to pay for the pizza. She should've thought about the cost before she agreed to feed five growing teenagers, not to mention one grown man. But when Clay had suggested the pizza, her only thought was making sure Max knew that his friends were welcome in their new home.

She was relieved when she managed to find two tens and a twenty-dollar bill in her purse. It was enough to pay for two large pizzas and give the delivery boy a tip. But this was going to set her back. She had just spent most of her paycheck on her tuition and school clothes for Max. Things were always tight on an aide's salary, but they would get by somehow.

Max grabbed the pizzas. The other kids followed him into the kitchen. As Beth headed that way, she remembered her car. Her stomach took a dive, and she stopped abruptly. How was she going to pay to get that car fixed? She barely had enough money for pizza, and she didn't get paid again for two weeks. Worry filled her mind.

"Problem?"

Beth turned to find Clay right behind her. The sinking sensation she had experienced a moment ago doubled as she looked at him. She didn't know whether the feelings came from his presence or the worry that he might suspect her dilemma. Either way, she just wanted to be somewhere else. She tried to smile. "I suddenly remembered my car. I forgot about it while we were moving and unpacking."

"You'll have to call a tow truck in the morning. Do you have a place that services your car?"

Her stomach sank further. A tow truck. Another expense. "No. I just buy gas where it's cheapest and use one of those quickie oil-change places."

"I could check around for you."

Why was he being so nice? What was in it for him? She hated being suspicious, but in her experience everyone was out for something. What were his motives? "Thanks, but I don't want to keep you from your own work."

"That's not till Monday. I've got the whole weekend free. I can see if someone at the church could help you out."

"But I'm not a member."

Clay smiled. "That doesn't matter. Christians are here to help *everyone*."

Beth bit her lower lip and studied the floor. What could she say? She had to admit that the people she'd met from this church were different than the church people she had known growing up. She didn't know how to react to their kindness. She feared that reaching out to them could eventually come back to bite her. Looking up at him, she shrugged. "For now, let's have some pizza."

Without waiting for a response from Clay, she hurried toward the kitchen. The five teens sat around the table and gobbled pizza while they laughed and talked. Beth stopped and watched. The best part of the evening was seeing Max having a good time with his friends.

"Hey, Mrs. Carlson, what kind of pizza can I get you?" Ryan jumped up and grabbed a plate.

"I'll take a slice of pepperoni." She didn't bother to correct the *Mrs.* That would only cause confusion.

Ryan scooped a slice from one of the boxes and put it onto the plate. "Here you go." He handed it to her. "How about you, Mr. Reynolds?"

"I'll take the same. Thanks." Clay picked up a plate.

Ryan placed a slice on the plate and then pulled out a chair. "Would you like to sit here?"

Clay shook his head. "We old folks are going out to the porch to enjoy the nice evening. Right, Beth?"

Wishing she could say no, she stared at him. If she protested, she would appear foolish. "Sure."

This was not what she had planned. She followed him out the door. Without waiting to see where he might sit, she perched on the porch steps. She put the plate on her lap, picked up the pizza and took a big bite. She savored the melted cheese and sauce. Maybe a full mouth would give her an excuse not to talk.

"You ever see reruns of *Leave It to Beaver?*" He settled next to her.

She nodded, her mouth still full of pizza.

"That Ryan reminds me of Eddie Haskell, the kid who sucked up to the parents but was always cooking up trouble when they weren't around. What do you think?"

Shrugging, Beth swallowed hard. The bite of pizza

went down in a big lump, it and Clay's presence making her stomach churn. Although he wasn't touching her, his nearness surrounded her like an invisible force. A tight pressure gripped her chest, and for a moment she forgot to breathe. Finally releasing a slow, shaky breath, she surveyed her new neighborhood. Streetlights shining on the trees cast long shadows as dusk crept across the landscape. Lamps illuminated windows up and down the quiet street. If only the peaceful setting would calm her inner turmoil. "I don't know him. So I can't make a judgment."

"I'd keep my eye on him. I've noticed that when he thinks no grown-ups are watching, he acts kind of wild. He could be a problem."

A disapproving voice from the past echoed through her mind. Her father had said a similar thing about Max's dad. Her father had been right, but his judgmental attitude had driven her right into the arms of Scott Harkin. "I've taught Max to be polite. So if he's courteous, will you think he's sucking up?"

"I wasn't suggesting that. I just thought you might want to watch this Ryan's influence on your son."

"I want Max to have friends."

"But you want him to have the right kind of friends, don't you?"

"Yes, but they ought to be friends of his choosing."

"Sometimes kids don't always make the right choices."

"That's true, but suggesting that he stay away from Ryan might make his friendship that much more appealing."

Clay nodded. "I can't argue with that."

Finishing off the last bite of her pizza, Beth thought

about the choices she had made. Did Clay surmise that she had made bad ones? Was he thinking like mother, like son? She didn't want to care what Clay thought. It wasn't any of his business anyway. She peered at him in the waning light. "What makes you such an expert on teenagers?"

"My past."

"What about it?"

"I was like Ryan. I could lay it on thick for the adults, but out of their sight I was a troublemaker."

Beth took in that information. *Well, this was a surprise. Mr. Christianity had a past. A past that went with his motorcycle and long hair?* "Would you care to explain?"

"Let's just say sometimes I wonder how I managed to live past my twenty-first birthday. Compared with me, Eddie Haskell was a model citizen."

"Just because you were like that doesn't mean Ryan is."

"Yeah, but I'd still watch him."

"I'll keep your warning in mind." She didn't want to argue. Should she be more suspicious of Max's friends? Being with these kids had caused him not to come home on time. But then they had helped with the move. She shouldn't borrow trouble. Did she dare ask Clay what had changed his life? If she did, he'd probably preach at her. She didn't want that.

Picking up his plate, Clay stood. "I'm going to get another slice of pizza. You want one?"

"Sure." She handed him her plate. As he took it, their fingers brushed. Her pulse hammered. He smiled. Could he tell the effect he had on her? Probably. Scott Harkin with his motorcycle had been trouble, but Clay was trouble of a whole new sort. He would no doubt use his charm and good looks to convince her she needed God. Maybe she did, but she doubted that God wanted her. She had spent most of her life pushing God away. When she had asked Him for help, He hadn't been there. That wasn't going to change.

Clay parked his motorcycle in front of the Petits' house. He jogged up the front walk and took the steps two at a time. Standing on the porch that went across the entire front of the white clapboard house, Clay punched the doorbell. He hoped Brian could help Beth with her car.

After a few moments Kim opened the door. "Hey, Clay. What brings you by?"

"I came to see Brian."

"He's out back in the garage."

"Thanks. I'll head that way." Clay started down the steps, then stopped and turned. "How are Jillian and the baby?"

"They're doing great and coming home this afternoon. You're invited to the baby shower we're having a week from Thursday evening out at their place."

"I thought you gave showers before the baby was born."

"The shower was supposed to be tonight, but the baby came early, so we had to postpone it."

"And another thing. Aren't showers for women?"

Kim laughed. "Not these days. Guys are included, too."

"Have they picked out a name?"

"Jillian wants to name the baby after Sam, but he's not sure he wants that." Kim chuckled. "We'll see who wins."

"Any suggestions for a gift?"

"Maybe if you ask real nice, Beth will help you find one."

"I'll keep that in mind." He continued down the steps. "See you later."

While Clay walked around the house, he wondered whether Kim was trying to do a little matchmaking. Didn't it matter to her that Beth didn't seem to accept God? Maybe Kim was just trying to get more Christian influences into Beth's life. When Clay reached the garage, he spied Brian with his head under the hood of a car.

The smell of oil and grease greeted Clay as he stepped into the dimly lit building. Along the walls, tools hung on Peg-Board in neat arrangements. A workbench sat under the window that looked out over the carefully manicured backyard where a wooden jungle gym occupied a corner. Clay grinned at the thought of the Petits' twin six-year-olds. Those boys were bundles of energy. Flower boxes filled with a rainbow of petunias sat in each window of the house and garage.

"Hey, Brian. Working hard?"

Brian looked up with a smile. "Just tinkering."

"I thought I'd heard that you worked on cars."

"A little."

"Enough to replace an alternator?"

"Sure, why?"

"The alternator on Beth's car went out yesterday after you left. I don't think she has the extra money to get it fixed. I was hoping we could help her out."

Brian picked up a nearby rag and wiped his hands on it. "I'll see if I can track down an alternator for the make and model of her car."

"I'll pay for it, if you donate the labor."

Brian nodded. "Have you run this by Beth?"

"No. I wanted to check with you first before I mentioned it to her."

"Let's go into the house, and I'll make some calls." Brian let the hood of the car slam shut.

Clay followed Brian through the backyard and into the house. While Brian sat at a round oak kitchen table, much the same as Beth's, he made some phone calls. Clay waited impatiently as he ran a hand along the countertops that gleamed in the late-morning light. Floral-print curtains ruffled in the breeze coming through the window above the sink. The tantalizing smell of a freshly baked pie filled the room. The signs of domestic bliss assaulted his mind. Sometimes when he saw family settings like this, he wanted the same thing. But then he remembered his itch to keep moving on, to march to the beat of his own drum, and the thoughts quickly fled.

"I've found an alternator for her car." Brian's statement shook Clay from his thoughts.

"Super. When can we get it?"

"My uncle said he'd bring it by after lunch."

"Will you call Beth and tell her?"

Brian wrinkled his brow. "She'll think it's strange if *I* call about the alternator. Why don't you call?"

Clay grimaced. "I'm not sure how she'd take it. Sometimes I get the impression she doesn't like me much or that she thinks I'm interfering."

"I don't know her that well myself yet. We'll let Kim do it."

"Let Kim do what?" Kim appeared in the kitchen doorway.

"Call Beth and tell her we're getting a new alternator for her car." Brian handed Kim the phone.

"She needs a new alternator?"

"Yeah," Clay replied, and he proceeded to fill Kim in on what had happened.

"I can't believe two big guys are afraid of calling one little woman." Kim chuckled.

"Who's afraid?" Clay asked. "I'm just being practical. She'll be more receptive to the news if you tell her. She already thinks I'm interfering in her life."

Shaking her head, Kim punched in the number. While she talked to Beth, Brian poured a couple of glasses of water and handed one to Clay. He watched Kim talking on the phone and tried to figure out from her body language how Beth was receiving their offer of help.

After Kim hung up, she grinned. "Beth is absolutely thrilled you guys want to fix her car." She turned to Clay. "I told her you needed help picking out a gift for the baby shower. She'll be glad to assist you."

"Thanks." Clay sighed. Was Beth really glad to help, or had Kim made her own interpretation of Beth's reply?

"Why did you say she thinks you're interfering in her life?"

"I probably overstepped my bounds the other night when I gave her this advice about Max and his friends," Clay admitted.

Kim went to the refrigerator and pulled out some packages of lunch meat. "When it comes to Max, Beth's protective instincts are ferocious. That boy means everything to her."

Clay nodded. "I could tell. What do you know about Max's dad?"

"Not much." Kim opened a loaf of bread. "Join us for

lunch, and I'll fill you in on what little I do know about Beth and Max."

"Thanks. Can I help?" Clay asked, wondering about his interest in Beth. Was he entertaining thoughts he shouldn't have? A relationship with a woman who didn't honor God could only lead to trouble.

"You can make your own sandwich." Kim handed him a plate. "I just get out the fixings."

He grabbed the plate and made a sandwich as he tried to shake the image of Beth's blue eyes. He had to keep her in perspective. She needed help. She needed to know God. What better way was there to show her God's love than to help her? Clay wanted to understand her better so he could share his faith with her. At least that's what he kept telling himself.

After they'd made their sandwiches, Brian said a prayer. The three ate in silence for a few moments until Kim looked pointedly at Clay. "What did you say to Beth about Max's friends?"

Clay recounted his experience with Max and his buddies and explained what he had said to Beth. "That probably wasn't the wisest thing to do with someone I'd just met."

"You might be surprised," Kim replied. "She may have given you the impression she didn't like your interference, but I bet she welcomed your advice. It's not easy raising a kid alone—especially a boy."

Clay shrugged. "She told me her father was a preacher. Why is she so set against God?"

"I'm not sure. She doesn't say much about her past. You asked about Max's dad. In the two years I've known her, Beth told me he's dead but didn't offer any details."

"Was it a recent death?"

Kim shook her head. "I don't think so. The only thing I know for sure is she was sixteen when Max was born. And I know that only because I once saw her birth date on her driver's license and did the math."

"Wow. I thought she looked young." Clay rubbed his hand across his chin. "Was she married to Max's dad?"

"I don't have a clue." Kim shook her head. "She's never been very talkative, and I didn't think it wise to ask."

"Maybe that's why she doesn't have any use for the church?"

Kim nodded. "Could be. We had a situation like that in the church here last year. Jillian's nephew got his girlfriend pregnant. She was just seventeen. Dylan and Tori came before the church and asked for prayers and forgiveness. They did get married, and she finished high school before the baby was born."

"How did the members of the church react?" Clay asked.

Kim set her sandwich on her plate. "On the surface most people had an okay attitude, but I heard some unkind remarks from a few who thought there ought to be some consequences. Some punishment. I just thought, if God can forgive them, why can't we?"

"Yeah. We all make mistakes. Some of them are just more visible than others. I wish people could understand that. Just like that story in the Bible of the woman caught in adultery. We shouldn't be throwing stones." Clay smiled wryly. "Do you suppose the congregation will accept me? I was pretty rebellious growing up."

"I lived a little on the wild side myself. Kim's influence changed my life," Brian interjected with a nod.

"What did she do?" Clay looked from Brian to Kim.

"When we were in college, Brian asked me out. I told him no."

"Turned me down flat." Brian chuckled. "I finally got up enough nerve to ask her why."

"I told him I only dated Christian guys, but I would consider going out with him if he started going to church and agreed to talk with our pastor."

"You did that?" Clay furrowed his brow as he gave Brian a speculative glance.

Nodding, Brian reached for Kim's hand and gave it a squeeze. "I sure did. Just to get a date. I didn't intend to make that church thing a part of my life, but I discovered the love of God. My whole family did."

Watching this couple, Clay almost felt like an intruder. Their love for each other radiated from everything they did. He wanted to experience that kind of love. But with his lifestyle, was it possible? What did God have in store for him?

Some years ago, Jillian had been the same kind of influence in his life that Kim had been in Brian's, but it hadn't translated into a love match.

"That's a great story," Clay said. "So is that why you keep pushing me and Beth together?"

Shrugging, Kim gave him a sheepish grin. "I didn't think it would hurt. I've tried so hard to get her interested in church, but she resists most of my attempts."

Brian patted Kim's shoulder. "Yeah, my little matchmaker here was originally trying to entice Beth into going to church by introducing her to Sam."

"You mean Jillian's Sam?"

"Don't look so shocked. Jillian and Sam had broken

up years ago, and she'd left town. They got back together when Jillian moved home." Kim laughed. "So what about you and Beth?"

"I'll help her out, but that's as far as it goes. Besides, she's not interested in me," Clay replied, not wanting to give any hint that Kim's matchmaking might be working on him.

"Why do you say that?" Kim asked.

Clay shrugged. "Just the way she acts around me."

"Well, I hope you'll invite her to church sometime. I want her to experience the love of God." Kim took a bite of her sandwich.

"We can just keep showing her kindness. Like fixing her car." Brian smiled at Kim. "Maybe she'll finally see God's love through us."

"That's what I've been doing, but I get frustrated that she won't let God back into her life. Something bad happened in that girl's past," Kim said.

Clay eased back in his chair. "If she had a lousy experience with church, maybe she's afraid of what will happen if she gets too close. It can take just one unkind remark to undo a lot of good."

"You've got that right." Kim nodded. "We just have to keep praying and being her friends."

Clay popped the last bite of his sandwich into his mouth. Friends. Could he be just friends with Beth when that wistful smile and those expressive blue eyes made his heart feel too big for his chest? He would have to make that a matter of prayer as well.

On Thursday evening Beth drove up the steep gravel driveway leading to the Lawsons' house outside of town.

When she pulled to a stop, she couldn't help noticing the motorcycle parked near the house. Her heart skipped a beat. Clay was already here. Should she have offered him a ride? Probably, but she feared the proximity. Kim had told Beth he needed help finding a baby gift, but he had never asked her. She'd halfway hoped that meant he wouldn't show at the shower. Every time she looked at him, her stomach tied itself into knots. Pushing aside her negative thoughts, she grabbed the package wrapped in blue-and-white paper and marched toward the front door. She punched the doorbell. While she waited for an answer, even the peaceful pine-woods setting didn't calm her stomach.

Kim answered the door. "Hey, Beth. I'm glad you made it."

"Thanks to Brian's work on my car." Beth smiled and handed the package to Kim.

"He was glad to help out. Let's join the party." Kim headed for the living room. She glanced back at Beth. "Sam and Jillian and baby Sammy will be so glad to see you."

"I'm eager to see the baby."

"I may be prejudiced because he's my nephew, but I think he's the cutest thing."

Following Kim, Beth gripped her purse strap as though it were a lifeline. Groups of people always made her nervous. Well, adults anyway. A classroom full of kids was a breeze.

Guests were scattered throughout the living room with the stone fireplace that reached to the vaulted ceiling. She smiled and nodded at several folks she recognized from town. Nearly everyone in attendance had something to do with her friends' church. While she followed Kim through the room, Beth wondered about the thoughts behind the friendly smiles. Did they see her as some kind of sinner because she didn't attend services with them?

Near the wall of windows looking out onto the pines, Jillian sat holding the baby, who was wrapped in a blue blanket. She was involved in an animated conversation with a young woman who balanced a squirming toddler on one hip.

As Beth drew closer, Jillian glanced up. "Beth, I'm so glad you came. It's good to see you. Are you settled in your new place?"

Beth nodded, acknowledging the genuine greeting. "Yeah. I'm fine. Your baby is adorable!"

"Thanks. His daddy sure is proud." Jillian looked at Sam, who stood on the other side of her chair, talking with another man. She touched his arm.

He turned. "Hey, Beth. Glad you came. Sorry we had to leave with the job half done the other day, but—" he paused and looked down "—this little guy was eager to get here."

"You don't have anything to apologize for. Max and some of his buddies and your friend Clay finished unloading the furniture." What would she have done without Clay? He had stepped in to help despite her less-than-enthusiastic acceptance. She didn't understand why.

"Did I hear someone talking about me?"

Beth looked up into a pair of twinkling gray eyes. Her heart jack-hammered. Her mouth went dry.

"Yes." Jillian smiled. "Beth mentioned how you

helped her move. Now you can help her find a place to sit. It looks as if Kim's ready to get the festivities started."

"Sure." He put a hand to Beth's back. "How about here?"

Breathless, she could only nod. She swallowed hard. He had her tongue-tied and weak-kneed. Thankful to get off her wobbly legs, she sat in the chair he pulled out for her. When he settled into the chair next to her, she closed her eyes for a moment and willed away her reaction to his presence. She wouldn't allow herself to be sucked in by a good-looking face and broad shoulders.

While Jillian opened gifts and passed them around for everyone to see, Beth pondered the unconditional acceptance she was receiving from these people. Everyone was so friendly. They didn't shun her because she didn't go to church, but would they if they knew the whole story of her past? She didn't want to find out.

Despite her obvious reluctance to join them, they included her. Even when she repeatedly turned down invitations to attend worship services, they continued to be her friends. She tried not to speculate about their motives, but she couldn't help wondering why they bothered with her. One thing was obvious. They loved and cared about one another. She wanted to be part of that even if she remained on the fringes. Sometimes their constant caring almost drew her in, but she feared their rejection if she got too close.

Beth watched Jillian and Sam. He held baby Sammy while she opened gifts. The joy and pride on his face made Beth's heart ache. Max had never had a father who was proud or joyful over his birth. No one had given her a baby shower.

Her parents had never seen their one and only grand-child. She remembered their judgmental, unforgiving attitude when she had told them she was pregnant. They had called her a shameless unwed mother and immediately shipped her off to stay with her great-aunt. Her dad was afraid of how her condition would affect his ministry. They wanted her to give Max up for adoption, but Beth loved Max from the moment she first held him. She couldn't bear the thought of giving him away. When she refused to give him up, her parents severed all ties with her. She hadn't seen or spoken to them in fifteen years.

Beth shook away the bad memories as Jillian finished opening the gifts. Then Kim indicated that everyone should enjoy the refreshments. Beth followed the crowd toward the table set with a cake and punch bowl. Cake and punch and conversation. The cake and punch were easy. The conversation was not.

She picked up a glass of punch and a plate with a small piece of cake. Weaving her way through the crowd, she searched for an out-of-the-way corner. While she sipped her punch and nibbled the cake, her thoughts took her back nearly sixteen years to the day when she had told Max's dad she was pregnant.

She had called him and said she would meet him at the library, where she often sneaked away to see him. He picked her up there and sped her off on his motor-cycle toward the edge of town to an abandoned farm-house, the place he always took her to end their dates. As soon as they stepped into the empty building, he grabbed her and kissed her.

She pulled away. "Stop, Scott, I've got something to tell you."

"What's that, babe?"

She hesitated, her heart pounding.

"Well, what? Spit it out."

"I…I'm pregnant."

Scott stiffened. "Can't be my kid. I used a condom every time we did it. You must've been with some other guy," he'd said coldly.

Tears welled in her eyes, and she took a shaky breath. "No, I've never been with anyone but you. I love you. I thought you'd want to get married."

"Marry you?" He laughed. "That kid's not even mine."

"Yes, it is. Condoms sometimes fail, you know."

"Yeah, well, even if it is my kid, I'm too young to get married. I have plans. And they don't include a wife and kid. I'm going to college. I won't be hanging around this burg." He laughed again.

The cruelty of his words tore at her very soul, and she swallowed a huge lump in her throat. The sob she'd been holding back escaped. "You…you said you loved me."

"Grow up. Why'd ya think I said that?"

"Because you love me!" Her own desperation sounded in her ears. He *had* to love her. How could it be any other way?

He took her by the shoulders. "Hey, this was just for fun. It was a dare—that I could make it with the preacher's daughter. Too bad it had to end this way, but it was fun while it lasted, right?"

Numbness kept her from crying. A dare? Fun? How could she have been so stupid? Who was this guy? Not the person she had dreamed about every night. Not the person to whom she had entrusted herself, heart and body and soul. Everything he had said about loving her forever was a lie. All of it. A lie. Her parents had warned her, but she hadn't believed them. They had been right all along. Fear squeezed her heart. "This is your baby, Scott. You must care. You have to help me."

"Yeah, I'll help you. Help you get rid of it."

In a daze, she rode with him to an ATM. He withdrew money from his account and shoved the bills into her hand. "Here. Get an abortion. And don't bother me again."

An abortion? *Never.* It was her only thought as he drove her back to the library. Clutching the bills in her hand, she watched him ride away as her heart plunged into her stomach.

A touch on her arm startled her back to the present. "You look lost in thought, hiding here behind the potted plants."

Beth looked up. Her gaze met an earth-shattering grin. She managed to smile. Another good-looking guy who rode a motorcycle. Why couldn't Clay Reynolds just go away and leave her alone? Then maybe her heart wouldn't pound and her mouth wouldn't go dry and every coherent thought wouldn't drain out of her brain.

"Hi." Brilliant conversation. Now what could she say?

"Nice place Sam and Jillian have here."

"Yeah." Small talk. She hated it. She wasn't good at it. Why couldn't he go talk with someone else?

"Are you looking forward to the first football game tomorrow night?"

"I guess so."

"I never did get around to giving you those football instructions."

"That's okay." She shrugged. "I'm basically just hoping Max won't get to play. Then he can't possibly get hurt."

"Max probably doesn't see it that way, right?"

"Right. He likes to kid me. He made me promise not to run onto the field and tackle the other team myself. He thinks I'm a worrywart."

"You might be." Clay grinned and patted her arm. "What's Max doing tonight?"

"He's studying," she replied, hoping he couldn't tell how his touch made her pulses throb.

"Sam told me Max used to attend some of the church's youth group functions. They'd love to have him back at their gatherings."

"Yeah, well, he's been busy with football practice." Didn't Clay get it? Or was he being intentionally obtuse? She had told him she didn't have any use for church. She hated making excuses for why they didn't attend worship services, but that didn't change the way she felt. She didn't understand why these people continued to pursue her when she had made it perfectly clear she wasn't interested.

"I'm going to help Sam out with the youth program while I'm here. I'd like to have Max join in some of the activities."

"You'll have to ask him about that. It's his choice," she said, wondering what would happen if Clay invited Max to attend a church function. She was probably the only mom in town who'd worry that her son *would* go to church. But she had her reasons.

"Good. There's going to be a party at the church for the kids after the game. I'll see if he wants to come."

"Fine." She gazed out the window at the dark clouds gathering above the treetops. What did she say now? She wasn't sure how she felt about Max's getting involved in church again. When she and Max had first moved to Pinecrest, Kim had instantly befriended them and invited them to church. Max had attended some of the youth functions, and since she had wanted him to make friends, she hadn't discouraged him. When he lost interest, she didn't care. All along she feared he would be ostracized as she had been.

"You don't sound as if it's fine."

She turned to look at him and willed away any reaction to him. "You know how I feel about church. But I'm going to let Max make his own decision."

"Okay. That's fair." Clay turned toward the window. "Looks like we're in for a little rain."

"If it rains, won't you get wet riding home?"

He grinned at her. "Not if you give me a ride."

How could she turn him down when he had been so much help to her? "What will you do with your bike?"

"Park it in Sam's garage. So, will you give me a ride?"

"Sure." She didn't want to give him a ride, but after everything he'd done for her, she didn't know how to refuse his request. The mere thought of having him so close on the fifteen-mile trip into town had her stomach tied in knots. It was bad enough that Kim kept pushing Clay at her. Now even the forces of nature seemed bent on the same thing. As if to punctuate her thoughts, a few raindrops pelted the windows.

"Looks like I'm going to need that ride."

Chapter Four

Clay forced himself to look out the window instead of at Beth. Maybe if he stared at the rain long enough, he could wipe her adorable image from his brain. Her expressive eyes held him captive even when they seemed to say *I wish you'd go away.* Women didn't usually resist him or just plain ignore him. Was that what made Beth Carlson so fascinating? The challenge? Better purge that idea from his brain. But Clay couldn't deny his reaction to her.

"Beth, how's your car running?" Brian's question stopped Clay's straying thoughts.

"Fine. Thanks to you."

"And Clay here." Brian clapped Clay on the shoulder.

Looking at Brian, Clay shrugged. "You did all the work."

"Well, let's say it was a team effort." Brian turned his attention back to Beth. "Kim wants to know if you can stay after the shower and discuss the school's fall festival."

Beth glanced at Clay. "Can you get a ride with someone else?"

"I could, but I don't mind waiting," he replied, wondering whether he had imagined her expression changing from one of relief to irritation. "I'll use the time to talk with Sam about the football party."

"If that's what you want." Beth smiled, but even her smile seemed to say *Please find another ride. I don't want to spend more time with you.* She scurried toward the front door, where Kim was saying good night to the other guests.

Clay observed from a distance as Beth shrank into a corner while she waited for Kim to finish her farewells. Several people filed past her with a nod or smile but didn't stop to converse. All the guests seemed intent on getting to their cars before it started to rain harder.

"Glad you were able to come tonight. Try not to get too wet," Kim called while she held the door open.

After the last guest left, Kim closed the door and leaned against it. Closing her eyes, she emitted a loud, satisfied sigh.

Before Beth could step forward, Brian sauntered into the entryway and gave Kim a big hug and kiss. Then he held her at arm's length. "You did a great job tonight, hon."

"Thanks. Did you talk to Beth? I barely saw her."

"She's right here admiring the potted plants again." Clay winked and gave her a wry grin.

Beth looked at him with a frown. "I thought you were going to talk with Sam."

"He's helping Jillian put Sammy to bed," Clay replied.

Kim eyed him speculatively. "You'd be a good candidate."

"Candidate for what?" Clay wrinkled his brow.

"Beth needs another guy in the festival's Dunk the Hunk booth," Kim replied.

"Oh, no, I don't think so." Clay shook his head and looked in Brian's direction. "Why not Brian?"

Brian held up his hands. "They've already recruited me. It's for a good cause. They're raising money for new playground equipment."

"Come on, Clay. Brian's right. Do a good deed." Kim picked up some plates and headed for the kitchen.

"I'm sure there are lots more well-known guys in town who'd be a better draw to a dunking booth than I'd be."

"Clay's right, you know. We need people the kids know." Beth hurried past him. "I'm sure we can find someone else."

"Someone else for what?" Sam asked, entering the kitchen behind Clay.

"The festival's dunking booth," Brian answered as he began washing dishes.

"I'm trying to convince Clay to fill one of the 'hunk' slots." Kim walked over and patted him on the back.

Laughing, Sam used his hands as if framing a picture. "That's a great idea. I can just see it now. Clay soaking wet after I hit the bull's-eye."

"Don't get too smug. I haven't agreed to anything yet."

"Chicken?" Sam eyed Clay.

"Hardly." Clay glanced at Beth and got the clear impression she didn't want him to be involved. For some reason she didn't like him, but he was determined to change that. Would helping out put him on her good side or bad? There was only one way to find out. Agree to be in the booth. "I accept your challenge. I'm going to volunteer just to see how good an arm you've got." Clay playfully chucked Sam on the shoulder. "And I get first crack at Brian and Sam when they're in the hot seat."

"No promises on who gets first crack at any of you." Kim shook her head. "Beth's in charge, and I'm sure she'll take tickets on a first-come, first-served basis. Right, Beth?"

"I don't care who's in the booth just as long as someone is." Beth gazed at Clay, and he couldn't mistake the flash of irritation in those blue eyes.

"And after the festival Brian and I are having all the festival workers over to our house for a cookout."

Clay leaned against the snack bar. "Hey, this is sounding better all the time. A free meal."

"Seems to me you recently *had* a free lunch at our house," Brian joked.

Clay shrugged. "What can I say? I'm not much of a cook."

"Maybe you and Beth can trade lessons. She'll teach you about cooking, and you can teach her about football," Kim chimed in while she put a few plates into the dishwasher.

He didn't miss Beth's frown at the suggestion as she helped clear away leftovers from the counter. It was becoming quite obvious that Kim's intention was to push Beth and him together at every opportunity. And from his perspective, Beth clearly indicated her displeasure with that situation. He wanted to change her attitude, but he didn't know how. Maybe just leaving her alone was the best answer.

"Now that you mention football, Sam, we should talk about tomorrow night. And you ladies can discuss whatever you need to about your school festival." Clay turned toward the living room, hoping to think about something besides Beth.

* * *

Watching Clay disappear around the corner with Sam and Brian, Beth slapped the cover onto a blue plastic container full of leftover cake. Why couldn't Kim mind her own business? Beth suspected Kim was again trying her hand at matchmaking. Her attempts two years ago to get Sam and Beth together had failed. At first Beth had entertained the idea, because the attractive teacher and part-time youth pastor had captured her attention. But she knew Sam would never be interested in her once he really knew her. A preacher, even a part-time one, wouldn't countenance her past. Then Jillian Rodgers had moved back to Pinecrest, and any thoughts of Sam's interest were quickly dispelled.

Max had looked up to Sam when they first moved to Pinecrest, and Beth suspected he wished Sam could be his dad. But Max had changed a lot in the past year, and his interest in Sam and the youth group at church had waned. Max wasn't that same gangly new kid hoping to make friends—or her little boy—anymore. Sometimes it made her sad to think how fast he was growing up.

"Did beating on that container help?" Kim asked.

Beth jerked her head up. "Help with what?"

"Clay."

"Did I say anything about Clay?"

Kim chuckled. "You didn't have to. I saw the look on your face and the way you took your displeasure out on that container. What's your problem with him?"

"I don't have a problem *with him*." Beth paused and put a hand on one hip. "I have a problem with you trying to push us together. It makes me feel awkward because it puts him on the spot, too. He's probably thinking, oh,

I have to be nice to poor Beth Carlson because her friends keep shoving her at me."

"Nobody's shoving you at him." Kim leaned on the counter and eyed Beth. "It was his idea to help with your car."

"Then he thinks I'm a charity case."

"I doubt that."

"I know his type. He's not used to women not falling for him at first sight."

"How can you say that? You barely know him."

"You don't know him that well either, do you?"

"Well enough," Kim protested.

"Know who?" Jillian walked into the room.

"Clay," Kim answered.

"Did you get the baby down for the night?" Beth asked in hopes that the conversation would veer away from Clay.

"At least for a few hours. I usually have to get up a couple times in the night to feed him." Jillian walked over and gave Kim a hug. "Thanks so much for throwing the shower."

"I loved doing it."

Jillian glanced from Kim to Beth. "So why are you two talking about Clay?"

Beth sighed. So much for changing the subject. She busied herself with the cleanup and hoped she could avoid the discussion. *Yeah, right. Like that was going to happen.*

"Beth thinks I'm trying to push her and Clay together," Kim responded in Beth's silence.

"She's probably right. You do have a tendency toward matchmaking," Jillian said.

"Only when necessary." Kim gave Jillian a perturbed glance.

Jillian laughed. "I guess I can't complain. She did a pretty good job with Sam and me."

"Well, I'm not interested in her matchmaking." Beth slapped another cover onto a plastic container.

"Protesting a little too much?" Kim raised her eyebrows.

"No." Sighing, Beth shook her head. "He's not my type."

"I can understand that." Jillian smiled. "He's a great guy but not my type either. I'm not sure who'd be a match for Clay. He's a rolling stone. Owns only his motorcycle and laptop and rents the rest. He likes to travel light. That's why he was so perfect to take over short-term until Maria joins us in November."

"Who's Maria?" Beth asked, hoping to steer the conversation away from Clay for good.

"My friend Maria Sanchez," Jillian answered. "She used to help me run the foundation until we moved up here from California. She's doing mission work in El Salvador right now."

Finally the conversation centered on something other than Clay. But he still wasn't far from Beth's thoughts. Despite her earlier protests, the information she'd gleaned about Clay bothered her more than she wanted to admit. He was definitely a "temporary" guy. She would keep that firmly in mind when her hopscotching heart betrayed her sensible thoughts regarding him. She wouldn't think about him anymore tonight. But how was that going to happen when she had to give him a ride home?

Clay watched from the doorway while Beth sat at the kitchen snack counter and talked with Kim. She smiled readily and gestured with her graceful hands. If only she could be that at ease with him. He wished he could figure out what he had done to earn her disdain. Maybe he should simply ask her. Would the direct approach work? *Lord, give me the wisdom to deal with Beth in a way that would open her heart to You.*

Approaching her with caution, Clay stopped near the kitchen table. When Kim glanced his way, he asked, "Are you ladies finished?"

"Yeah, she's all yours." Kim glanced at Beth.

Hopping off the bar stool, Beth pressed her lips together. Her expression told Clay she was not amused at Kim's comment, no matter how innocently it was meant.

"Do you need to put your bike in the garage before we leave?" Beth asked.

Clay shook his head. "Already done. We can leave whenever you're ready. You got an umbrella?"

"No." Beth's expression grew grimmer.

"I'll lend you one. Follow me. I've got a spare in the entry closet." Jillian hurried toward the front door and located an umbrella.

Clay took the umbrella and turned to Beth. He hated the fact that she looked as if she was going to the dentist rather than giving a neighbor a ride home. What would it take to change that look? He shook the thought aside, realizing this could easily get to be an ego thing with him. He shouldn't care about her opinion of him, but he did. He opened the front door and stepped onto the covered porch. Rain poured off the roof and splattered onto the walk. He opened the umbrella. "Ready?"

Nodding, Beth joined him. "Okay."

The way she gave her one-word response left no

doubt that she wasn't comfortable with the situation. Maybe he should have found another ride home. Why was he letting this woman tie his ego into knots? He was making this too much about himself and not enough about God.

Glancing back at Jillian and Kim, who stood in the doorway, Clay waved. "Good night." He turned to Beth as he stepped under the umbrella. "Care to join me?"

She took a deep breath. "Guess I don't have a choice."

"Not unless you want to get soaked." For an instant he was tempted to walk off without her, but he smiled instead.

She waved at Kim and Jillian. "See you guys tomorrow for the game." In a flurry of good-byes, Beth stepped under the umbrella and glanced up at him. "Let's go."

"Huddle close or you'll get wet." He had the urge to put an arm around her waist and pull her near him, but that would be an insane thing to do.

As they dodged puddles that reflected the yard light, they crossed the gravel driveway. Their shoulders brushed when they stopped at the car. Trying to ignore the way the contact made his insides flutter, Clay opened the driver's door. Beth slid under the steering wheel, and he closed the door. After he got into the car, she drove toward the main road. The headlights pierced the darkness and illuminated the streams of rain pelting the windshield. The hum of the motor, the ping of the rain and the swoosh of the wipers sounded loud in the silent interior.

Clay sat there and tried to think of something to say. Nothing came to mind. This was nuts. He usually didn't have trouble talking with women. What was wrong with him? The weather was usually a safe subject. He cleared his throat. "Does this area usually have these temperature extremes in such a short period? A week ago it was a hundred and six, and tonight it's probably snowing on Mount Spokane. Is the weather always this crazy?"

Beth shrugged. "I don't know. I've only lived here a couple of years."

Well, so much for that topic. Maybe football. After all, she did need to know something before she watched Friday's game. "I heard you say something about the football game to Kim and Jillian. Are you still dreading it?"

"Yes." She continued to look straight ahead.

"If you don't want Max to play, why did you let him go out for the team?"

"I want him to have the opportunity to try what he enjoys."

"Even though it makes you nervous?"

"Yes, because when I was a kid I didn't have the chance to do the things I wanted to do."

"And why was that?"

"We moved a lot, and my parents had certain ideas about what was appropriate for girls and what wasn't." Biting her lower lip, she glanced his way, then back at the road.

Clay wondered how much more she might reveal if he asked. Would she open up to him about her past? Maybe he could tread lightly and get some answers. "What did you want to do that they deemed inappropriate?"

She didn't speak for a moment, but that little smile he had seen before curved her lips. "I wanted to play softball. I would've been good, but we moved before I had a chance to try out. Not that my parents would've let me. But I used to sneak away and play ball with the neighborhood boys."

Clay chuckled. "I'll have to tell Sam. He'll recruit you for the church softball team. It's coed."

"Don't tell Sam anything. I'm not interested in softball anymore. I don't have time for games."

"We all need to have a little fun once in a while."

"Well, my fun revolves around Max. I'll let him be the athlete in the family." She reached over and turned the knob on the radio. Pop music blared from the speakers. She turned down the volume. "I hope you don't mind a little music."

"I don't mind," Clay replied, knowing this was her way of putting an end to the conversation. Somehow he had to find a way to break through the barrier she had erected against him. Or maybe that barrier was against anyone who tried to get too close.

"Are you ready to cheer for Max if he gets into the game tonight?" Kim asked as they walked across the parking lot amid the crowd headed toward the football field.

She shuddered. "No, I keep picturing him in a heap on the ground with a dozen huge guys piled on top of him." Beth gazed at the floodlights illuminating the field. Her stomach churned. Out of the corner of her eye she caught sight of Clay heading toward them. His presence didn't do a thing to calm her nervous stomach. She took a deep breath and released it slowly. "Why couldn't he have been interested in soccer?"

Chuckling, Brian gave her shoulders a squeeze. "He'll survive."

"Just wait till your boys are old enough to play

football," Beth replied, trying to take her mind off her own worries.

"I've thought of that, too." Kim grimaced, then smiled. "But I remind myself that Brian and Sam both played football. They never got seriously hurt. So let's be positive."

Brian nodded. "That's right. Sam and I played and lived to tell about it."

"I played football, too," Clay added, joining the group. He held his arms outstretched. "See? I'm in one piece."

Despite her churning stomach, for some reason looking at Clay tonight and hearing his reassurance made Beth want to smile. She bit her lower lip, forced the smile away and put on her most serious expression. "But what did all that pounding do to your brain?"

"I managed to graduate from law school, if that's any consolation." Clay grinned at her teasing, then turned to Brian and Sam. "What about you guys? Any ill effects?"

Brian shook his head. "We both got through college."

Beth sighed. "Okay, you guys. Quit making fun of me."

"We're not making fun. Just trying to ease your mind and lighten your mood so you can enjoy yourself and not worry so much." Brian gave her shoulders another squeeze.

Beth tried to glare at the three men, but a smile crept across her face. She looked at Kim and Jillian. "How do you deal with these guys?"

"We just ignore them," the two women chorused and then laughed.

Beth joined in the laughter as the group made their way into the stadium and onto the bleachers. Moments like these made her want to throw aside her reservations and share their faith. But fear always overrode that yearning to fully step inside their world. Critical voices in her mind told her she wasn't good enough to stand with these people despite their seemingly unconditional acceptance of her.

While Beth's thoughts whirled, she followed the group to a prime spot on the fifty-yard line. When they settled on the bleachers, she found herself sandwiched between Kim and Clay. There was no point in letting the seating arrangement bother her. She had to learn to deal with Clay and with Kim's attempts to be a matchmaker. The gregarious talking, laughing and an occasional shout filtered into Beth's consciousness. She tried to concentrate on everything except Clay and the way their shoulders brushed every time he leaned over to say something to Brian. Applause and cheers broke out as the Pinecrest Wildcats ran onto the field. They broke through a huge paper banner held up by the cheerleaders while the band played the fight song.

There was Max, number eighty-two, taking his place on the sidelines. A lump rose in Beth's throat when she saw her son, looking so grown-up in his blue-and-gold jersey and shoulder pads. Pressing her lips together, she blinked back a tear. Pride filled her heart. She swallowed a lump in her throat. The band played the national anthem. The names of the players in the starting lineups boomed over the loudspeaker.

"Having a good time yet?"

She looked up into Clay's twinkling gray eyes. They spelled mischief. Or was that her imagination? "I think so."

"Nervous?"

"Not yet." At least not where Max was concerned. He

wasn't in the starting lineup. Did Clay suspect that *he* made her nervous?

"Good." He smiled. A smile that seemed to say *I understand.*

Beth smiled in return, and her heart melted a little. She didn't want to like this guy. He reminded her too much of Max's father. Scott had sucked her into his web of deceit so easily. She had fallen for his smile and smooth lines. Maybe Clay was different. Yeah. He was different, all right. His smiles and smooth lines had a completely different motive. He wasn't out to win a bet or get her into his bed. He was using his charm and attention to get her back into church. Of that she had no doubt.

A roar erupted from the stands, shaking Beth from her thoughts. The teams took their places on the field. Everyone stood for the opening kickoff.

"Do you know what's happening?" Clay gave her a curious glance.

"The game's getting ready to start," she replied, hoping he didn't think she was completely stupid. She gave herself a mental shake. Why did she care what he thought? One of the opponents kicked the football. A player from Pinecrest caught it and ran a few yards before he was tackled and lay at the bottom of a pile of bodies. Cringing, Beth closed her eyes.

Clay chuckled and touched her arm. "You can open your eyes now. No one was hurt."

"Don't laugh at me." She shuddered. "I don't know whether I'll be able to watch if Max gets into the game."

"Would you like me to explain what's going on?"

"Okay." She forced herself to look at the field again as the players formed two lines on either side of the ball.

Clay started to explain what was happening on the field. "Right now the two teams are at the line of scrimmage. That's the line the ball is set on. When Max comes into the game, he'll be a receiver."

Before Clay could go on with his explanation, the players began to move. Beth lost sight of the ball, and in the next instant there was a big pile of players on the field again.

She took a deep breath. "I don't get it. I can't keep track of the ball."

"Just keep watching. It'll get easier."

Beth doubted that. She glanced over at Kim, who was completely engrossed in the action on the field. When the next play unfolded, Beth watched Kim's reaction. Without warning, everyone jumped up and started yelling. Beth looked back at the game. One of the Pinecrest players was running down the field with a player from the opposing team in a black-and-red jersey in hot pursuit. The crowd roared until the opponent caught the Pinecrest player and tackled him.

"All right!" Kim gave Brian a high five, then turned to Beth. "A first down."

"Is that good?" Beth asked.

Nodding, Kim chuckled. "Yeah, didn't Clay give you those football instructions?"

"No." Beth shrugged. "I didn't have time."

Oddly enough, now she wished she had let Clay give her those instructions. But she had been afraid to spend more time with him. So she had made excuses about being too busy or too tired. While she ruminated over her decisions to avoid him, another play unfolded, resulting in yellow flags flying in the air.

"What are the yellow flags?" Beth asked.

"There's a penalty. In this case offsides," Clay replied. "Someone crossed the line of scrimmage before the ball was snapped."

"There's too much to figure out in this game."

Giving her arm a pat, Clay proceeded to explain the rules and the penalty. "You'll get it."

Steeling herself against his touch, Beth nodded. "I suppose."

After a couple of more plays, the crowd was once again standing. Beth glanced around. "What's happening now?"

Clay waved a hand toward the field. "Pinecrest is about to score. They have the ball inside the ten-yard line. If they get the ball over that solid white line at the end of the field, they make a touchdown and score six points."

Beth tried to follow the ball, but she always lost track of it until the play was over. "Did they score?"

"No. They have the ball on the two-yard line." Clay hunched over her shoulder. "Watch closely this time. I'll try to help you follow the ball."

A crescendo of cheers rose as the teams lined up again. Despite the difficulty of concentrating with Clay standing so close, she saw the player with the ball cross into the end zone. She joined the uproarious cheers and applause. She hadn't felt this lighthearted in a long time. As the game progressed, Clay's instructions finally began to make sense. When the first half ended, the score was tied at fourteen.

During halftime, Beth accompanied Kim and Jillian to the ladies' room and then to the concession stand. As they waited in line, Kim leaned over and whispered, "Looks like you and Clay are hitting it off."

Beth wanted to protest, even though she had to admit she was actually having a good time. But she didn't dare let Kim know. "He's explaining the game to me. That's all."

"Well, that's a start."

"The start of nothing."

"We'll see." Kim laughed and stepped up to place her order.

While they made their way back to their seats, Beth realized she had missed all this during her high-school years because she had dropped out of school. She didn't want Max to miss anything. If his participation in sports and church activities meant putting her fears aside, she would do it. Despite her vow, when the game started again, she still breathed a sigh of relief as Max remained on the bench.

During the second half, Beth became so engrossed in the game that she didn't mind Clay's presence beside her. His careful instructions made her forget that she didn't want to like him. When the Pinecrest Wildcats scored another touchdown, she realized Clay had penetrated her defenses just like the Pinecrest team had run through the defensive line of their opponents. The cheering crowd brought her back to her senses. She couldn't fall for another good-looking guy with ulterior motives, no matter how nice he seemed.

At the beginning of the fourth quarter, Pinecrest scored another touchdown. Their opponents hadn't scored in the second half. The time ticked away on the scoreboard at the end of the field. Every minute that passed eased Beth's worry that Max might get into the game. She finally began to relax as she watched the cheerleaders along the sidelines. Beth recognized Brittany and Lisa as they performed a tumbling stunt. Watching the two girls made Beth remember how fast Max was growing up. Was she prepared to talk to him in depth about girls? The prospect brought a flutter to her chest. Without a father, how was Max going to know about being a man? A good man.

While she let her thoughts run afield, she failed to notice that the Pinecrest team was ready to score. When the crowd rose to its feet, she joined them. Cheers thundered as the play developed. In seconds Pinecrest scored another touchdown, and shouts of joy exploded from the stands. In the next series of downs, Pinecrest held their opponents to an eight-yard gain, forcing them to punt the ball.

As the Wildcats' defense came off the field and the offense returned, Kim tapped Beth on the shoulder. "Look. There's Max. He's going into the game!"

Beth's stomach filled with butterflies as she saw number eighty-two run onto the field. She turned to look at Kim. "Why?"

Brian leaned over. "Because they have a two-touchdown lead, the coach is giving everyone a chance to play."

"But I don't want him to play." Swallowing hard, Beth bit her lower lip.

Kim patted her arm. "It'll be okay. Max must be excited to be in the game."

As the next play progressed, Beth couldn't take her attention off her son. Her heart pounded as he ran down the field. The play ended near the line of scrimmage, and she was thankful Max wasn't involved. The seconds continued to tick off the clock as the teams lined up for the next down. Again Max ran and the play ended without his involvement. She closed her eyes.

"I think he'll live," a male voice whispered in her ear.

Beth jumped and placed one hand on her chest. She looked at Clay. In her concern over Max, she had forgotten Clay was there. "You scared me."

He chuckled. "I thought you were more afraid of what was happening on the field."

"Don't kid. This makes me nervous." She sighed again.

"Okay, but I think Max would love to get his hands on the ball."

"Maybe so, but I'd rather he didn't."

Clay waved a hand toward the scoreboard. "You may get your wish. Time's running out. And it's third down and six yards to go. If they don't make a first down here, the other team gets the ball."

Beth held her breath while the teams lined up again. The center snapped the ball. The quarterback dropped back. He threw the ball. Beth was excited that she recognized the positions and the moves. Max would be so proud. Then her mind spun as she watched the ball spiral through the air toward number eighty-two. Not an opponent near him, Max extended his arms and snatched the ball. Turning, he headed toward the goal. He sprinted down the field. Two opponents raced after him.

Screaming and hollering with the crowd, Beth jumped up and down. When Max crossed the goal line untouched, relief coursed through her body, and her heart soared with pride. Her son had scored a touchdown. Tears of joy welled in her eyes. In her exhilaration, she threw her arms around Clay. He returned the hug so exuberantly that her feet left the bleachers. After he set her down, heat rose in her cheeks as she realized what she had done. Not daring to meet his eyes, she instantly turned to give Kim a high five. High fives and congratulations flowed from Brian, Jillian and Sam as well as from folks sitting nearby.

She basked in her son's accomplishment—until she remembered Clay. She had thrown herself at him. How stupid. What must he think? If only a big hole could open up in the bleachers and she could drop out of sight. How could she turn around and face him?

Chapter Five

Once their impromptu embrace had ended, Clay found himself staring at the back of Beth's head. Her light hair, falling in soft waves around her shoulders, shone in the stadium lights. Her startled expression and the pink tinge of her cheeks before she turned away left little doubt that she was embarrassed. So now she was ignoring him.

Max waved amid the cheering students who had rushed onto the field at the end of the game. Beth returned the greeting by waving her hands wildly above her head. She still kept her focus on the field as Max and his teammates trotted toward the locker room.

Trying to calm his thumping heart, Clay remembered the way Beth had felt in his arms. Soft, supple and all woman. She had fit perfectly into his embrace. He purged the thought from his mind. Romantic notions about this woman were off-limits. She didn't share his faith. Besides, he wasn't going to get tied down in this tiny town. He had to remember these facts when he looked into her bright blue eyes and had second thoughts about his plans.

"Hey, Clay, that was quite a game, wasn't it?" Sam's question stopped Clay's thoughts short.

"Yeah. Great game." He glanced at Beth. She still wasn't looking his way.

"Max looked good making that touchdown." Turning to Beth, Sam patted her on the shoulder. "And here's the proud mom."

Beth beamed at Sam's comment, but she still didn't look Clay's way. Why should she? He was reading way more into her embrace than he should. She had simply been excited about Max. That was the only reason.

But Clay couldn't shake the idea of wanting her hug to mean more. More about him and less about Max. A completely ridiculous—not to mention ungenerous—thought.

"Let's head over to wait outside the locker room for the players." Brian ushered Kim ahead of him. "Then we can congratulate Max."

"Sounds like a good idea." Clay resisted the urge to grab Beth's hand and race toward the exit where the players would emerge after they showered and changed.

"Hey, guys, I'd love to do that, but I've got to get over to the church before the kids arrive for the get-together," Sam said as Jillian slipped her arm through his.

"Okay, we'll see you there later." Clay waved along with the others as Sam and Jillian headed toward the parking lot. Clay glanced at Beth. "I didn't get a chance to talk to Max about the party. Did you mention it to him?"

"No." She shook her head. "I thought you were going to."

"Yeah, I was, but I never ran into him. I'll ask him

when he comes out." Clay tried to gauge Beth's reaction, but he couldn't read her expression. The exuberant woman who had embraced him in the bleachers had disappeared. The shy, quiet woman so familiar to him had returned—the woman whose normal demeanor indicated that she wished he wasn't present. That bugged him more than he wanted to admit.

She shrugged and turned to Kim as if to dismiss him.

Clay tried not to let her dismissal bother him. He joined Brian and some of the parents who were reliving the Pinecrest victory while they waited for their children. Finally the football players began to come through the doors. Proud bystanders applauded.

When Max appeared, pride beamed from every inch of Beth's smile. The six-footer leaned over and gave his mom a quick hug. Then Ryan and Alex, the two boys from moving day, appeared at his side. A conversation ensued that Clay couldn't hear. Before he could ask Max about the church teen gathering, Max gave Beth another hug and sauntered away with Ryan and Alex.

As the boys disappeared into the dim light, Clay hurried to speak with Beth. "Where's Max going?"

She turned and looked at him with the familiar expression that told him she had once again forgotten his presence. "The guys from the team are going to Ryan's house. I told Max he could go as long as he was home by midnight."

"Oh, well, I missed my opportunity to invite him to the party at church, then." Clay shook his head.

"I don't think he would have gone anyway," Beth said.

Clay wanted to kick himself for not making a better effort to talk with Max. Now he was off with Ryan and his buddies. Clay didn't have a good feeling about the kind of gathering that would ensue. Had Beth thought to ask about the presence of parents? Of course she had, Clay chided himself. But even if adults were there, sometimes they looked the other way while their children did whatever they wanted. Clay stopped himself from asking questions. He shouldn't interfere with how Beth dealt with her son. Even though he feared what might happen, he had to remind himself that it wasn't any of his business.

"Do you have any plans?" he asked before he thought. Then he realized that he had hoped Max would come to the church because he wanted Beth there also.

"Yeah. I'm going home to study."

"I thought your classes hadn't started yet."

"They haven't, but the syllabus for the course is up on the professor's Web site, and I want to get started."

Now what could he say? She had a good excuse not to join them at the church. Her son wasn't going, and she needed to study. "Well, good luck with your studies. I admire your discipline."

She lowered her eyes as the pink tinge returned to her cheeks. "Thanks. Well, I'd better get going." She looked at Brian and Kim. "I'll see everyone later."

As Beth started toward the parking lot, Clay stayed at her side. "Let me walk you to your car."

She turned and gazed at him in the dim light. "You don't have to do that."

"I'm going that way." He fell into step beside her.

When Beth didn't get that distant look on her face that he so often saw when he offered to help, his hopes soared. Maybe she was beginning to like him just a little. He tempered that thought with a reminder that this wasn't about him. This was about being a witness for God. And something told him he was going to have to remind himself of that fact every time she looked at him.

He stood by her car while she unlocked it. After she removed the key, he reached around her and opened the door.

"Thanks. I hope your teen thing at church goes well," she said.

"I'm sure it will. I'm just sorry Max won't be there. I'll make sure I catch him next time. Would you let him know I'd like to talk to him?"

"That's between you and Max. I'm not getting involved." Beth slipped behind the steering wheel.

"Okay. Do you mind if I try to catch Max when he comes home tonight?"

"That's okay with me."

"Great. We'll be done at eleven-thirty. I'll stop by. I should get there just about the time Max does."

"See you later," she said. Still not meeting his gaze, she closed the car door.

Clay watched her drive off and tried not to question his eagerness to see her again.

Clay parked his motorcycle in the garage and sprinted to the house where he took the back stairs two at a time. He wanted to freshen up before he went to see Beth. Glancing at his watch, he knew he had about twenty-five minutes before Max was due to arrive home. He unlocked the door to his apartment. Before he stepped inside, the sound of a car engine made him turn.

The headlights of a dark blue Jeep illuminated the alley as it stopped just short of the garage. The back passenger door closest to the house opened, and someone stumbled out. The door shut, and the vehicle sped away. Streetlights still dimly lit the area. Clay watched the figure stagger to the garage, lean against it and bend over. A retch sounded in the quiet night. A moan followed.

Someone was sick.

Clay tossed his helmet inside the door and closed it. He raced down the stairs. When he drew near the garage, he recognized Max. Still leaning over, he didn't see Clay approach.

As the boy slowly straightened, Clay couldn't miss the glazed look in Max's eyes. The kid was drunk.

Disappointment charged through Clay's mind. What should he do? Surely it would break Beth's heart to see her son like this. Worse, she would probably blame herself for being a bad parent.

Wiping a hand across his mouth, Max started to stagger away. Clay grabbed his arm. The smell of alcohol and vomit reached his nostrils. The smells brought back memories of his own wasted youth. Would Max have to make all the same mistakes he had? Not if he could help it.

"Leave me alone." The boy's words were slurred as he jerked his arm away. "I suppose you're going to snitch to my mom."

Clay let his hand fall to his side. "What do you plan to do, Max? You think you can fool her? I won't have to tell her anything. She'll see for herself."

Max leaned back against the garage and hung his head. "I don't want that," he mumbled.

"Maybe you should've thought of that before you got drunk."

"Yeah, well, don't do me any favors. I can take care of myself."

"Doesn't look that way to me." Clay glanced at his watch and then once again reached out to put a hand on Max's arm. "You still have twenty minutes until your curfew. I can help you clean up."

Max gave Clay a skeptical look. "And why would you do that?"

"Because I care about you and your mom. I would hate for her to see you this way."

"You mean you wouldn't tell?"

"I'm not sure what I'm going to do yet. That might depend on you."

"How's that?"

"Come on up to my apartment, and we'll talk about it."

"I suppose." Max pushed himself away from the garage, his eyes unfocused yet wary as he weaved his way toward the steps.

Clay followed closely in case the kid stumbled and fell. As Clay opened his door and ushered Max into his living room, he wondered how he was going to handle this. *Lord, I'm not sure how to deal with this situation. Help me not to make matters worse.*

"Are you still nauseated?" Clay asked.

Max shook his head, his face pale. Embarrassment replaced his wary expression. "What do you want me to do?"

Surprised by the boy's sudden acquiescence, Clay once more took his arm. "First let's get you cleaned up. The bathroom's right down this hall."

A little steadier on his feet, Max made his way into the bathroom. Clay stopped in the hallway to pull a towel and washcloth from the linen closet. He stood in the doorway and handed them to Max.

"Can you manage?"

Again Max nodded. Suddenly the kid looked very young and very scared. "Are you going to tell my mom?"

"I'm still not sure what I'm going to do. Let's just say your cooperation will make things a lot easier on you."

"I'll do whatever you say." Max seemed contrite.

Clay leaned against the doorframe and watched while Max turned on the water in the sink. He stuck his hands under the faucet, then leaned over and sloshed water onto his face.

"I'll give you some privacy, and I'll think about what I intend to do. After you get yourself into some kind of reasonable shape, come out to the living room. We'll talk about it."

"Okay." The word came out muffled from behind the washcloth.

Clay made his way to the kitchen, where he rummaged through a cupboard for some instant coffee. After finding a jar stuck back in a corner, he heated a cup of water in the microwave. The timer beeped just as Max entered the living room.

"Have a seat." Clay gestured toward the sofa, then stirred coffee into the steaming water. He doubted the coffee would have much effect, but it was worth a try. Time was the only thing that cured drunkenness. He'd learned that lesson well.

"Now what?" Max asked as Clay approached, carrying the hot coffee.

"Drink this." He handed the cup to Max. "And listen."

The boy held the cup and stared at Clay, eyes filled with fear. Max was alert enough now to know he was in big trouble. "You're going to tell my mom, aren't you?"

Clay slowly shook his head. "I don't want to. I'd hate to see the disappointment on your mother's face when she finds out. She was so proud of you tonight at the game. I'd hate to take that away from her."

Max brightened. "So you're not going to tell?"

"I didn't say that. I just said I don't want to."

Max took a big gulp of coffee and remained silent.

"I'm going down to your place with you." Clay glanced at his watch. "In about five minutes."

"Won't my mom think that's strange?"

"No, I told her I would stop by after the church function."

"Why?"

"Because I wanted to talk with you."

"About what?" The belligerence returned to Max's voice. He took another drink.

"About attending the church get-together after the next home game."

"I bet you aren't interested in having me there now."

Clay shook his head. "Not true. Now I want you there more than ever. In fact, I expect you to come."

"Why? I won't fit in."

"What makes you say that?"

"Because they don't want me around."

"Who's they?" Clay asked, his brow wrinkling.

"People."

"What people?"

"Church people."

"Kids?"

Max shook his head. "No. Some old lady at church."

"What happened with the lady at church?"

Max took another sip of the coffee and then looked at Clay. "When we first moved here, I went to some church stuff 'cause Mom's friend Kim invited us. But I overheard some lady saying something about my mom and me. She didn't want her grandchildren hanging out with a…with an illegitimate kid."

"I'm sorry she said that. That woman was wrong. I know my saying it probably doesn't help much, but she was very wrong." Man. The woman's statement hit Clay almost as if it had been directed at him. Didn't church folks understand what it meant to be a witness to those outside the church? Hadn't they ever read the story of the woman caught in adultery? "Your mom said you quit going to the youth functions. Is that why?"

Taking another gulp of coffee, Max drained the cup, then nodded.

Clay took the cup to the kitchen sink. He returned to Max, who still sat on the sofa. He looked a little better, a little more sober. Some color had returned to his cheeks.

"Time to go." Clay looked at his watch. "On the way downstairs I'll tell you what I plan to do."

"Okay." Max followed Clay to the door.

"We're going to talk to your mom together. If she suspects your condition, you are going to confess everything and ask for her forgiveness. You got that?"

Max paused on the bottom step. "But what happens if she doesn't suspect?"

"Then I'm not going to 'snitch,' as you say. But here's the deal. This better not happen again, because I'm going to be watching you and watching you good. You understand?"

"Yeah." The kid nodded.

When they reached the back door to Beth's apartment, Max tried the door. It was locked. He fished his key out of a pocket in his jeans, then unlocked the door. He let it swing open, then eased his way across the threshold. Clay joined Max just inside the door. Only the steady hum of the refrigerator greeted them.

Max tiptoed through the kitchen into the dining room. Clay closed the door and followed him. Max stopped abruptly, causing Clay to almost knock him down.

Straight ahead, Beth sat on the sofa with a book in her lap. Her head lolled to one side. Clay's heart fluttered at the sight of her sleeping. He motioned for Max to go to his room. Clay followed and shut the door behind them.

Max stared at him. "Are you going to wake her up?" he whispered.

"Yes." Clay nodded. "I'm going to tell her you're in bed. So get ready now."

"Okay." Max stared at Clay while he clutched the door leading to the bathroom that connected to his bedroom. His knuckles were white against the dark wood. "Are you going to tell her about tonight?"

"No point in it now, but remember our deal. I'll expect you at all the church youth-group activities from now on. No excuses. Are we on the same page?"

Max nodded while that wary look crept back into his eyes. "So you're not going to tell?"

"Let's just say I'm not going to volunteer the information. If your mother asks, I'll have to tell the truth."

"Please don't tell. I'll do whatever you say."

Compassion for Max trickled through Clay's mind. The kid had made a mistake, but he seemed truly repentant. Could Clay trust that Max would follow through on his promise?

"I have to wake her. We can't let her sleep in that position. Besides, if she wakes up later, you'll have to do the talking. Do you want that?"

"I don't know," Max replied with a shrug. "I really messed up this time, didn't I?"

"You did. Don't let it happen again."

"I won't. I promise."

"How you feelin'?"

"Better, but still not that good. At least I don't feel like I'm going to puke again."

"Good." Clay nodded. "You can sleep it off, but you might not feel that great in the morning, either."

"How would you know?"

Clay blew out a harsh breath. Should he tell the kid the truth? Yeah. "Because I've been right where you are. And believe me, it's not the place to be."

"You serious?"

"Yeah. And I'm not proud of it. There's nothing good about getting drunk. Now go brush your teeth and use mouthwash. Then get to bed, and I'll take care of your mom."

"I'm there." Max smiled for the first time since he'd come home. "Thanks."

"You're welcome. Just remember our deal."

"I will." Max disappeared into the bathroom.

Clay proceeded through the dining room but stopped between the built-in curio cabinets. Beth still slept on the sofa. The book had slipped from her lap and now lay against her leg and the sofa cushion. Her lips slightly parted, she breathed in a steady rhythm. A warm sensation filled his chest.

The urge to gather her into his arms and kiss her awake percolated in his mind. He closed his eyes and willed the thought away. He couldn't act on his attraction. He wanted to help Beth and her son; kissing her would only create more problems.

He tiptoed across the room and stood next to the sofa. Was he doing the wrong thing by not telling her about Max? Clay had to believe that Max would fulfill his promise.

Bending, Clay touched her arm. "Beth."

She jerked awake. Shaking her head, she blinked up at him. She put a hand over her heart and shrank back into the sofa. "What are you doing here? How did you get in?"

"I'm sorry. I didn't mean to startle you. Max let me in."

"Where is he?" Her gaze darted around the room.

"He's already in bed." Clay pointed to the boy's room. "He didn't want to wake you, but I thought you might get a kink in your neck if you slept there too long."

"When did he get home?" She picked up her book and hugged it to her as she sat up straighter. "I didn't hear him come in."

"He got home a little after eleven-thirty. I happened to get home at the same time. So I took the opportunity to ask him about attending the next youth get-together. We had a good talk, and he's planning to come back to the youth functions at church."

"He is?" Incredulity colored her words.

"Yeah. I hope that's okay with you."

"I said he could make up his own mind. It just surprises me." Beth stood, still holding the book. "He's sleeping?"

Clay nodded. "Yeah. He had a big night, and he seemed really tired."

"I'm so sorry I missed him! I'm going to check on him." She set her book on the desk as she passed through the dining room.

"Sure," Clay said, taking a long slow breath while he followed her to Max's room. Would she figure out what Max had been doing tonight?

She eased the door open and poked her head inside. Clay hovered behind her. The light from the dining room shone through the open doorway and across Max's bed. He lay there fast asleep, his hair dark against a white pillowcase. He must have fallen asleep as soon as he hit the bed. A soft snore resonated through the room.

She turned to Clay. "He *must* be tired. He never snores."

"Must be." Clay held his breath as Beth entered the room.

She stopped beside the bed and tucked the covers around her sleeping son, then bent to kiss his cheek. Max stirred but didn't awaken. She brushed his hair back from his forehead. Love for her child radiated from her face. For just a moment Clay wished that look was meant for him. He pushed the thought to the back of his mind. Crazy. Crazy. Crazy. He couldn't let himself go there.

Concentrate on the son. Stay away from the mother.

As he let those phrases replay themselves in his mind, Beth joined him in the doorway. "He's a good kid."

"Yeah." Clay gazed at her. "Then everything's all right?"

Nodding, she closed the door behind her. "I'd better get to bed myself. I certainly didn't mean to fall asleep before Max got home."

"What's he doing tomorrow?" Clay asked, wondering how the boy would feel in the morning.

"He has his regular Saturday chores." She narrowed her eyes. "You don't have some youth thing tomorrow, do you?"

"No, but there's a church campout up on the Pend Oreille River this weekend. It starts tomorrow. I'd like for you and Max to go."

"Max can after he finishes his chores if he wants, but not me." Beth shook her head. "I have a meeting with some of the PTA members tomorrow to work on stuff for the fall festival."

"That's okay. Lots of people aren't coming out until evening. You'd enjoy it."

"I doubt it."

"You don't like camping?"

She put a hand on one hip and grimaced. "You know what I don't like."

"Give it a try, Beth. You might change your mind."

"I gave it a try when I first moved here and Kim invited me to church. Nothing's changed. Besides, I don't have any camping gear."

"The way I hear it, there's plenty to go around."

"I don't fit in." She dropped her gaze as if to close the discussion.

Those were almost Max's exact words. Had Beth also heard that woman's unkind statement? Clay wanted with all the power within him to erase Beth's misguided feelings, but he didn't know how. He had to leave it in

God's hands. "Not true. I'd certainly like to change your mind. Give *me* a chance."

Pressing her lips together, she shook her head.

"Okay, I'll drop it," he said with a sigh. "Is it all right if I stop by to see Max in the morning? Maybe talk a little football?"

She shrugged. "If you want, but he has to get his chores done first."

"I'll make sure he does. Well, I'd better get going, so I don't keep you up. Sounds like you have a busy day tomorrow." Clay headed to the back door. He had to get out of there before his willpower failed him. Every time he looked at Beth, the thought of kissing her crept into his brain.

"I do. Thanks for the tips on football. I'm going to impress Max with my knowledge." A shy but genuine smile lit her face as she joined him at the back door. "Thank you, Clay. Have a good night."

"Good night."

He took the stairs to his apartment two at a time as if doing so would help diminish the effect her smile had had on him. He loved her smile. Her shyness. Even her stubbornness. Despite his resolve to focus on Max, he was going to have a hard time staying away from Max's mom. Even though she kept him at arm's length, something about her invited him to stick around. But sticking around was never in his plans.

Chapter Six

Clay awakened to the sound of a lawn mower. Rubbing his face, he glanced at the clock. Eight o'clock. He was getting a late start to the day, but then, he'd had a hard time falling asleep last night. His mind had buzzed with thoughts of Max and Beth. Especially Beth. He couldn't forget how she had looked last night as she slept. How she had so lovingly tucked her son into bed. And how she had smiled shyly and thanked him for his tutoring in football.

He didn't even want to think about the thing that haunted him the most. He had nearly kissed her when they said good night. Not a wise move. He was trying to show her God's love, not get personally involved with her.

He poured himself a bowl of cereal. While he ate it, he went to the kitchen window and looked out. The sun shone brightly in a cloudless sky. The sound of the mower grew louder. Max appeared, trudging behind the mower. He wore baggy jeans, an old T-shirt with faded writing and sneakers. A Seattle Mariners ball cap sat low over his eyes, which were already covered with sunglasses.

Clay smiled. Poetic justice. Loud noise and bright sunlight. Two things a hangover didn't need. Maybe this would serve to keep Max from repeating last night's performance. Clay prayed that it would.

When Clay finished his breakfast, he also dressed in jeans and a T-shirt. He loped down the stairs and stood on the porch. Despite the bright sunshine, cool morning air greeted him. He waved as Max mowed a new strip across the front lawn. Max waved in return but didn't smile. The strain on his face told Clay the kid had a *bad* headache. Clay had to give Max credit. He was out here doing his chores despite the previous night.

Clay continued to watch. He resisted the urge to check and see whether Beth was still at home. How was he going to spend time with Max and not get involved in Beth's life? For Beth's sake he had to guard against that possibility. Still, he needed to keep an eye on Max. Especially now. A hangover could impair his thinking. Not a good thing while he was operating a power mower.

A door slammed. Clay turned. Beth approached with her purse slung over one shoulder. Her blue knit shirt made her blue eyes even bluer, if that were possible. She smiled, and his heart pumped in rhythm with the *brrrr, brrrr, brrrr* of the lawn mower.

"Good morning. Off for your busy day?" he asked.

She nodded. "Just the morning. We should be done by lunch."

"Great. That means you can still go camping." He pointed over his head. "Cloudless sky. A great day for camping."

She glared at him, but he detected a smile lurking

behind her expression. "I thought we covered that subject last night."

"We did, but I thought I'd test the waters again this morning. You might have changed your mind."

"Not likely." Smiling, she shook her head. "Would you do me a favor, since you're going to talk with Max? Make sure he's doing okay. He seemed a little out of sorts this morning. I thought maybe he was coming down with something, but he insisted on doing the lawn. So I guess he's okay. But sometimes he just acts macho. He thinks he has to be the man in the family."

"You have a fine son there."

"Thanks." She smiled slightly, almost as if she was trying not to let him know how his statement had pleased her. "I suppose I'll see you later."

"You can count on it," he called after her as she hurried toward the garage.

Clay sat on the porch and read his morning devotion while Max continued to mow the lawn. After the boy made the last pass across the lawn, he shut off the mower. Chirping birds and the bark of a dog filled the silence left behind. Max removed the ball cap and leaned over the mower. After wiping his brow, he shoved the ball cap back onto his head.

"What's next?" Clay called to Max as he pushed the mower toward the garage.

Max stopped. "I have to clean my room and the bathroom. What's it to you?"

The belligerence had returned.

"I just wanted to see how you were doing."

"Why do you care?"

"Because I don't want you to make all the same stupid mistakes I made when I was your age."

"So you're going to be looking over my shoulder every minute?" Max resumed pushing the mower toward the garage.

"Pretty much." While doubt crept through Clay's mind, he followed Max. Had he made a mistake in not telling Beth what Max had done? Last night, protecting Max and Beth had seemed like the right thing to do. Today, with Max's attitude, Clay was having second thoughts. Why had he let himself get involved? A pair of brilliant blue eyes above a shy smile came to mind.

Max parked the mower in a corner of the garage. Then he turned and glared at Clay. "So if I do something you don't like, you're going to tell my mom?"

Clay stared back. Was this some kind of test? Did Max expect Clay to back down from their agreement? "I'm just going to make sure there are no repeat performances of last night. We had a deal. Are you backing out?"

"I can't make any promises." Max shrugged and walked out of the garage.

"You did last night?"

"Well, I don't remember a lot about last night."

"Let me refresh your memory." Clay joined the boy as he stepped onto the porch.

Max stopped in front of the back door. "Maybe I don't care to listen."

"Too bad. You're going to listen. I told your mom last night that you were planning to attend the church youth functions. That's what you promised me." Clay raised his brows. "What's your mom going to think when you don't do that?"

"She'll think I changed my mind." Defiance painted every word.

Clay sprang between Max and the door. What had gotten into this kid? Was he fighting back out of fear? Embarrassment? Distrust? "Hey, I'm not going to argue with you about this. Either you cooperate, or I tell your mom just what happened last night."

"I don't care. Tell her." Max made a move to go around Clay into the house. "Get out of my way. I have work to do."

Clay had no idea what to make of the about-face Max had made since last night. "Okay, Max, I may not be your father, but I won't let you talk to me that way."

"What way?"

"You know what I'm talking about. I'm sure your mom has taught you to respect adults. She's going to be disappointed all the way around with your behavior."

"How do you know?"

"Because I know."

"Yeah, well, you might think you do, but you don't know me or my mom. So leave me alone."

A sickening sensation hit Clay in the pit of his stomach. He didn't want to have to tell Beth about Max, but he didn't have a choice now. Max had backed out on his promise. Now Clay had to enforce his side of the deal, or he would surely lose all moral stature, if he had any, in Max's eyes.

Clay stepped aside. "Okay, if that's the way you want it. I'll be waiting right here to talk with your mom when she gets home."

Max made no comment as he entered the house, slamming the door behind him. Clay didn't miss the way Max had grimaced at the banging of the screen door. The kid was definitely hungover. Maybe that explained his attitude.

Clay stood on the porch and stared out at the yard. The smell of freshly mowed grass still hung in the air. He couldn't figure out Max's attitude. It was as though he was trying to anger Clay, no matter the consequences.

With a heavy sigh, he climbed the stairs to his apartment. He grabbed the daily newspaper and some files Jillian had given him to read. Then he descended the stairs to the porch. The perfect weather made for a great morning to spend outside waiting for Beth. But this was one time he wasn't looking forward to their meeting.

Clay's seat at one corner of the porch let him observe the front and back doors to Beth's apartment at the same time. Max couldn't leave without being seen unless he climbed out a window. Clay hoped that wouldn't be the case, but after his conversation with the boy, Clay had to consider every possibility. For the moment the sound of a vacuum cleaner told Clay that Max was busy at work.

Eventually the vacuum stopped, and Clay could only guess at what Max was doing. He glanced at his watch. Barely ten o'clock. He couldn't concentrate on the newspaper or the stuff from Jillian. His upcoming meeting with Beth played across his mind as he rehearsed what he intended to say. How should he deal with this situation?

Prayer. Yeah. Why had he let that be his last resort? Here he was trying to show Beth about God, but he had forgotten to lean on God himself.

Lord, help me out here. I want to show Beth and Max how You can be a part of their lives. Give me wisdom and the right words to say to Beth. Soften Max's heart.

After praying, Clay focused his attention on the sports page of the newspaper. He read the article about last night's game. Max got a mention. Had he seen the article? Had Beth? Clay wanted to share the article with Max but feared the kid wouldn't be receptive. And how would Beth react when she learned about Max's wild night? Despite the prayer, Clay realized he hadn't given all his worries to God. A sliver of worry still niggled at the back of his mind.

Before he started to pray again, the back door opened, and Max walked out carrying a bag of trash. Without noticing Clay, the boy trudged to the alley where the garbage cans sat. Still sporting the ball cap and sunglasses, Max, with his head down, shuffled back to the house. When he reached the porch, he glanced up.

He grimaced. "You gonna sit there and spy on me all day?"

"Who's spying? I'm enjoying the day and waiting for your mother." Trying not to let his irritation show, Clay stood and leaned against one of the columns that supported the porch roof. Max had played him for a fool last night, and he had bought it. He should have known better.

Max disappeared into the house without another word while Clay stewed over the boy's attitude. It broke Clay's heart. Was there any reasoning with Max? There didn't seem to be.

Just let it go. But Clay didn't want to do that. Maybe Max still doubted that Clay would tell Beth about the boy's drunken escapade. And maybe he thought he could talk his way out of it just the way he had wiggled his way out of trouble on moving day. Clay mentally kicked himself for the part he had played in that scenario.

While Clay studied the papers Jillian had given him, a car turned into the alley. He looked up just in time to see Beth drive her sedan into the garage. Taking a deep breath, he stood. Was he ready for this meeting? His mind reeled as she approached.

"You're still out here?"

He nodded. "Yeah, I wanted to be sure to catch you when you came home?"

Stopping, she gave him a wary look. "Not more camping propaganda."

"No, there's something we need to talk about."

"What?" She wrinkled her brow.

"It's about Max?"

"What about him?"

"Ah…I think he needs to be here when we talk."

"Okay, let's go inside, and I'll get him." She opened the door and stepped into the kitchen. "Max, I'm home. You got your work done?"

"Yeah," he called.

"Come here for a minute." Beth set her purse on the table and motioned for Clay to come in.

Clay stepped inside just as Max entered from the dining room. "Hey, Max. I'm here to talk with your mom. Are you ready to talk to her?"

Max no longer wore the sunglasses or the ball cap. The color drained from his face as he made a sudden stop in the doorway. "What have you told her?"

"Nothing yet. I wanted you to be here when we discussed it."

"What's this about?" Beth asked.

Max walked into the kitchen and parked himself in front of Beth. "The camping trip, Mom," Max replied before Clay could say a word. "We want you to go on the camping trip. Say you will. Please."

Trying not to let his mouth hang open in surprise, Clay took in Max's performance with a skeptical eye. What was the kid trying to do?

Beth turned to Clay with accusation in her eyes. "I thought you said this wasn't about the camping trip."

"I did, but I didn't know Max was going to bring it up." Clay raised his brows as he looked at Max. How to handle this? *Lord, help me here.* "What's the deal, Max? You told me only an hour ago that you didn't want to go on the camping trip. In fact, you told me—"

"I changed my mind. I thought about it and decided I really do want to go." The words tumbled out of Max's mouth as if he couldn't say them fast enough. "And I want Mom to go, too."

Clay weighed his options. Tell on Max. Or keep quiet and get both mother and son to the church outing. The decision wasn't easy, but could this situation bring Beth and Max closer to God? "What do you say, Beth? Max sure would like you to go."

"We don't have any camping equipment." She crossed her arms.

"Not a problem. I'm sure someone in the church has extras."

"I bet Kim and Brian do. They were chaperones for that camping trip I went on at the beginning of last summer." Max put an arm around his mom's shoulders. "Come on, Mom. Say you'll go."

Beth sighed loudly. "Oh, all right."

"You won't regret it." Max patted her on the top of her head. "Thanks. I'm going to get my stuff ready."

Beth stared after her son and then turned to Clay. "What just happened here?"

Shaking his head, he gave her a wry smile. "Your son just manipulated you big-time." *And me.*

"And you encouraged him." She continued to stand there with her arms crossed as she eyed Clay. "I think you put him up to that."

"Oh, no." Clay shook his head again. "This was all his doing. Believe me."

"Well, I'd better do some packing." Beth turned toward her bedroom.

"I'll call Kim and Brian and have them swing by and pick you two up. No need to take another car." Clay pulled a cell phone from his pocket, relieved that Beth had not asked why he wanted to talk to her about Max.

After making arrangements with Brian, Clay found Max tossing clothes into a duffel bag on his bed. "May I talk to you?"

Max glanced up. "I suppose."

Clay leaned against the doorframe. "What am I supposed to think? Would you like to explain?"

"Like I said. I just changed my mind." Max shrugged as he continued to pack.

"You know, Max, I'm not going to be able to trust a thing you say. How can I believe what you tell me after what you've done this morning? If you want my trust, you're going to have to earn it now."

Max stood with his head lowered while he kicked one sneaker against a bedpost. "I…I'll do that. I'll show you."

"We'll see. That's the same line you gave me last night. You have a lot of repair work to do as far as I'm concerned."

"I promise. You'll see." Max raised his head. That scared, lost-little-boy look Clay had seen the night before appeared in Max's eyes. Was it an act, or was his expression genuine? Was the boy a chameleon, changing to fit any situation as an act of self-preservation? Was he going along to get along? Was this another Eddie Haskell moment? Right scenario but wrong kid.

Or maybe Clay had had the wrong kid all along. How far could he trust this young man? How far could Clay trust himself to do what was right where Beth was concerned? Maybe the upcoming weekend held those answers.

Beth moseyed across the meadow at the edge of the ponderosa pine forest. She tried to convince herself she had agreed to come on this church camping trip to please Max, but she couldn't deny that her thoughts turned to Clay more times than she wanted to admit. Just looking at him made her heart flutter like the golden grass in the meadow waving in the breeze.

She pulled her jacket around her as the cool air made her shiver. Or was it thoughts of Clay that made her shiver? She shook the notion away. Why did she keep thinking about a man she didn't want to think about? His image flitted through her mind even when he wasn't there. Like now, when he was with the group that had gone to purchase fishing licenses and ice for the coolers.

Why had she let Max talk her into this? As she glanced across the meadow, she knew why. Max laughed and talked with a group of teenagers gathered near the dock. The river gleamed its reflections of the sun that hovered above the treetops in a cloudless sky.

Tents dotted the meadow. A group of campers and RVs sat closer to the road.

"Hey, what are you doing over here all alone?" Kim's question made Beth turn around.

Beth shrugged. "Just enjoying the scenery."

"Beautiful here, isn't it?"

"Yeah, especially the river."

"I'm glad you came. This is going to be a great weekend."

"If you say so."

Kim wrinkled her brow. "You aren't convinced?"

"I'm not much of a camper. And it's a little chilly. I'm not looking forward to sleeping in a tent."

"You and Jillian," Kim said with a chuckle. "She camps only because Sam likes it. They'll be up a little later tonight for the campfire."

"Jillian doesn't like to camp either?"

"That's right. But when you live in this area, you have to learn to love it. We go camping whenever we get the chance. Most of the church outings involve camping of some sort."

"I managed to live here for two years without having to camp."

"I don't know how we let you escape." Shaking her head, Kim pointed toward the far side of the meadow. "Let's go help the other women get things ready for supper. That ought to warm you up."

"Who does the cooking?"

"Tonight the women. Tomorrow night the men. I'll introduce you to some of the women."

"Sure." Beth followed Kim across the meadow.

Beth dreaded the introductions. They meant small

talk. Telling people about herself. Lots of new names to remember. All that was bad enough with regular people, but how would these church people look at her, the "bad girl" wandering into their territory?

The grass rustled beneath her sneakers. With each step she tried to tell herself it would be okay. As they drew near the women gathered around a cluster of grills, the smell of lighter fluid and burning charcoal lingered in the breeze, and narrow plumes of smoke curled heavenward.

"Hey, everyone, I'd like you to meet my friend Beth Carlson."

The women stopped what they were doing and looked her way. They smiled, and Beth managed to shove away the panic that threatened to take over her brain. Pushing at her glasses, she mustered a smile. "Hi."

In a flurry of introductions she met the entire group. She would never remember all the names, but they seemed friendly. For the moment she forgot to be nervous.

One of the women, a petite redhead with freckles dotting her face, stepped forward. "Hi, Beth. I'm Lori Gorman. I thought I'd introduce myself again, since you met so many of us at once."

"Thanks." Letting the tension drain from her shoulders, Beth smiled. "Do you have a job for me?"

"Sure. We need to get the chicken from the refrigerator in our fifth wheel." Lori pointed toward the RV camper hitched in the large pickup truck that sat closest to the grills. "It's right over there."

"That should be easy enough," Beth said as they made their way there.

"You're Max's mom, aren't you?"

"Yes. How do you know Max?"

"I don't, but my daughter Brittany does. She talks about him all the time."

The little redhead. The one who had helped with the move—and made Max forget his responsibilities. Was she here this weekend? Was she the reason Max had been so eager to go camping? "Yes, I remember meeting your daughter. She's a cheerleader, right?"

"Yes." Lori opened the door to the RV. "I'm glad you and Max could join us this weekend."

"I didn't see Brittany with the other kids." Beth took the boxes of chicken that Lori handed her.

"Oh, she isn't here yet. She's riding up with Sam. She had to go to cheerleading practice today. They're getting ready for a competition."

"That must be fun."

"Well, it is, but it's time-consuming." Lori carried the remaining boxes of chicken as she stepped out of the camper and closed the door. "So Sam said he'd bring her when he came."

Walking back to the grills, Beth wondered whether Max had known that Brittany would be here. She hoped not. Max was too young to be serious about a girl, wasn't he?

Yet Brittany was clearly thinking and talking about Max. And her mother didn't seem the least bit concerned. Or maybe the woman did have concerns and was checking out Beth as well as her son. When Lori Gorman found out about Beth's past, she would probably decide that her daughter should stay away from Max.

That would suit Beth just fine. Because if his own mother tried to put a stop to the relationship, Max would probably find the girl that much more of an attraction.

This whole scenario conjured up Beth's past like the smoke rising from the grills.

Well, maybe Lori had just as many worries about her daughter's getting involved with a boy. It was a legitimate concern. The temptations were everywhere. Even at a church campout. Well, Beth would be vigilant. Just because it was a church event didn't make it safe. Kids would be kids. She had been there herself. Despite all the teachings against premarital sex, teenage hormones ran strong. She knew from her own experience. And Jillian's nephew, Dylan, and his girlfriend—now wife— Tori, came to mind as well.

Sometimes teenage rebellion led to wild behavior, too. She herself had hated everything her parents preached. She didn't want that to happen between her and Max. But how did a parent walk the fine line between giving sound advice and turning off a lively child? Between setting rules and being too harsh?

She was beginning to see her parents in a new light. She didn't want to repeat their mistakes, but at the same time she wanted Max to know there were rules to follow to live your life the best way. And she worried about talking with Max about sexual matters because she herself was such a bad example. How could she tell Max what not to do when she hadn't followed her own parents' advice? Would he be convinced by her firsthand experience? Or would he consider her a hypocrite?

She wanted him to know how much she loved him and wanted only the best for him. And that was something she had never really felt from her parents. Everything had been negative with them. Don't do this. Don't do that. And the church had been that way, too. She had always felt she could never be good enough, so why try? She never wanted Max to feel that way. No matter what, she wouldn't fall into that trap.

Beth tried to keep her focus on the positive as she and Lori rejoined the other women. Soon the smell of barbecued chicken and baked beans wafted across the meadow. The men and boys began to set up picnic tables. The joyous laughter and squeals of children filled the air as they played tag. The camp's sounds and smells eased Beth's anxieties. Maybe this wasn't going to be so bad after all.

Turning around, she came face-to-face with Clay.

Or maybe not. He still made her heart race out of control. She had to deal with him, but she couldn't seem to speak.

"Hi there. I see you're joining right in." He carried a huge red-and-white cooler. "Where should I put this? It's full of soft drinks."

"You should talk to someone in charge, not me," Beth replied with a shrug.

"But I like talking with you." He winked.

Was he flirting with her? Why? Hadn't she made it perfectly clear she had no interest in his looks or his charm? Maybe that was the problem. Just like Scott, maybe Clay saw her as a challenge. Here was another fine line to walk. How could she discourage him without making his male ego react badly to rejection?

Beth didn't miss the way Clay's muscles rippled when he set the cooler on the ground. Berating herself for even noticing, she looked away. What was she putting herself through for Max's benefit? That boy had better appreciate this weekend. She glanced around the camp to find him. She spied him helping a group of guys stack wood for the campfire.

Her heart melted at the sight of him. Tall and handsome. Healthy. Happy. Her son. She sighed.

"Why the sigh?" Clay's voice startled her.

Her melted heart picked itself up and galloped around in her chest. Could he possibly hear it? She really wanted to scream, *Will you just go away and leave me alone if I admit that I think you're good-looking and that you make my heart flit around like the birds in the forest?*

She smiled instead. "Just taking it all in. It's so peaceful here." *Everything except you.*

"Glad you came?"

Maybe if she said yes he would go away, but she couldn't lie. "I'm reserving judgment."

"Well, at least you're not deciding to hate it before you give it a try." He continued to stand there, as if he expected her to say something else.

"Please excuse me. I have to help cook."

"How about helping me? I've got more coolers to move." He surveyed the ladies clustered around the grills. "Looks like they have enough workers. They won't miss you."

What could she say? His observation was true. Maybe trying to avoid him had been her problem all along. Was this the time to face the challenge head-on? If she quit avoiding him, probably her anxiety would evaporate into the pine-scented air. Yeah. Like that was going to happen. Oh, well, what did she have to lose, other than her peace of mind?

"Okay. What do you want me to do?"

"I'll show you."

She followed him toward a pickup truck. The tailgate was down, and more coolers sat alongside bags of ice. He jumped up onto the bed of the truck. He then turned and offered her a hand.

She stared at his outstretched hand. What was she worried about? She had thrown her arms around his neck and nearly tackled him in the bleachers at the game. Putting her hand in his should be a piece of cake after that.

"I'm not sure I can get up there."

"What's the problem? Afraid of heights?" he teased.

She put her hands on her hips. "Are you making fun of me?"

"No. Just wondering why you're procrastinating so hard."

She didn't dare let him know she was worried about holding his hand. He had her brain scrambled. What could she say?

"Hey, Mom, what ya doin'?"

Beth turned at the sound of Max's voice. She had never been so glad to see him. Relief washed over her. "I was going to help Clay load the drinks coolers, but now you can do it. I don't think I'm nimble enough to get up into that truck."

"Sure, you are. I'll give you a boost, and we can both help him." Max laced his fingers together and held them out. "Grab Clay's hand and step into my hands."

So much for being rescued by her son. He had joined the conspiracy against her.

"Okay." Holding her breath, she grabbed Clay's hand and tried not to think about the way his strong, callused fingers closed around hers. The warmth of his touch spread right up her arm. She focused her attention on stepping into Max's hands for the boost up. She held on tightly while Clay pulled her up. When her foot touched the tailgate, he grabbed her around the waist and steadied her.

"You made it." His face was so close, she could have kissed him by moving only an inch. Her chest filled with a warm fluttering sensation. She didn't dare move, despite the urge to stroke the strong jaw covered with a five o'clock shadow. She froze, fearful that she might give in to the temptation.

"Okay, what do we do here?" Max asked, hopping up behind her.

Beth jerked away from Clay. She had almost forgotten her son was even there. She had to get her head on straight before she did something stupid. Here she thought she was going to keep Max out of girl trouble, but instead she was getting herself into man trouble. Did her son have any idea that she was attracted to their new neighbor despite her best efforts not to be? And how would he feel if he knew? Better not to find out.

With Max's help, Beth and Clay filled the coolers with ice and drinks and delivered them to the picnic area. Just as they put the last cooler into place, one of the women rang a large school bell. Immediately people gathered near the grills, and one of the men gave a prayer of thanks for the food. Soon folks were filling their plates with chicken and a variety of side dishes.

While they went through the food line, Clay became engrossed in conversation with one of the other men. As soon as Max filled his plate, he went off with the other teenagers, who had staked out a table for themselves at the far end of the meadow. Beth saw her chance to escape temptation in the form of Clay. She glanced around looking for a place to sit. Seeing Kim at a nearby table, Beth headed that way.

"Hi, okay if I sit here?" Beth stopped next to the table.

"Sure." Kim patted the seat next to her. "Brian will be here in a minute. He's helping the boys with their plates. But then they'll be off with their friends."

"Thanks." Setting her plate on the table, Beth sat next to Kim.

"Where's Clay?" her friend asked.

"How should I know?"

"I thought I saw you two working together. Looked like you were getting pretty chummy."

Beth wanted to deny it, but she figured Kim would just keep badgering her. Better to just go along with her assessment. "Yeah. Max and I helped him load the drinks coolers."

"So, he's beginning to grow on you?"

Beth sighed. How could she answer that question? Just keep agreeing with Kim, and maybe she would be satisfied. "Sure."

Kim narrowed her eyes. "Okay. I get what you're doing."

"And what's that?"

Shaking her head, Kim chuckled. "I'm not even going to discuss it. Just eat. I think your buddy is headed this way with Brian."

Beth glanced up. Sure enough, with plates piled high, Clay and Brian approached. Thankfully, she sat at the end of the picnic bench, so he couldn't sit beside her.

But when he sat across the table from her, she decided that was worse. Every time she looked up from her plate, he was there. She couldn't ignore him. She managed to get through the meal by rarely looking up and chewing very slowly so she didn't have to talk. Conversation buzzed around her.

While they ate, the sun sank below the tree line. The evening sky was awash in pink and gold. The tall pines appeared black against the colorful backdrop. She drank in the beauty as she tried not to stare at Clay. But thoughts of him crossed her mind like the long shadows that crept across the meadow. The night air grew cooler. She shivered.

"You cold?" Clay asked.

She nodded. Here was her chance to escape. "I'm going to get a sweatshirt."

"I'll go with you." Clay stood. "I could use one, too."

Beth tried her best not to protest. "Where's your tent?"

"Right over there by yours." Clay pointed. "Didn't Max tell you he and I are sharing a tent?"

"No. But that's nice." Yeah. Real nice. Was Clay trying to be some kind of guardian? She didn't need someone to watch over her. Oh, what was she thinking? Of course, Max and Clay would share a tent. After all, she and Max were borrowing camping equipment. And she was borrowing trouble if she didn't quit letting Clay's presence bother her. "You know, on second thought I'm going to wait. I'll help with the cleanup, then get a sweatshirt."

"Okay." He waved. "See you at the campfire."

Brian got up. "Hey, Clay, wait a minute. I'll go with you."

The two men sauntered off as Beth began gathering

used paper plates. Clay didn't seem the least bit put off that she had rebuffed his effort to go with her. Maybe she was reading an interest into his actions that just wasn't there. All because her traitorous heart beat faster when he looked her way. She was becoming annoyed with herself for paying too much attention to *him*.

"Do I detect a little irritation?" Kim wadded up napkins and tossed them on top of the paper plates.

"About what?"

"You're always trying to play ignorant with me when you know perfectly well what I'm talking about." Kim placed a hand on one hip. "I'm finding the interaction between you and Clay quite amusing."

"Well, I'm so glad I can entertain you."

"Me, too." Kim chuckled. "You two remind me of Jillian and Sam."

"Did I hear my name?" Sam joined them at the table.

Kim turned. "Hey, how's my big brother? Where's Jillian?"

"She decided not to come. Sammy was cranky tonight, and she didn't want to leave him. Besides, you know how much she doesn't like to camp."

Kim chuckled. "Yeah. Like Beth here. But Clay managed to talk her and Max into coming."

Sam glanced Beth's way. "Hey, Beth. Good to see you. Max is here, too? Super. Even if you don't love to camp, you'll have a great time."

"That's what I told her." Kim gathered more trash. "The guys are down by the campfire if you want to join them."

"Yeah, I'll do that." Sam waved as he left.

Beth took the distraction of Sam's arrival to scoop up the remaining plates and napkins and head for the trash bins. No more insinuations from Kim. No more talk about Clay.

Surveying the campground, she spied the group of teenagers still sitting at one of the picnic tables. Max sat on the end. He laughed at something someone said. Thankfully, he was having a good time. That's why she had come. She forced herself to walk on to the trash bins and not stop to make sure Max was warm enough. Surely he would be embarrassed if she went over there now. He was old enough to know whether he needed a jacket. Letting go was so hard, but she couldn't always hover like an overprotective mother.

With that thought firmly in place, she scurried toward the tents to get a sweatshirt. She turned back to look at Max one more time. Worry worked its way into her thoughts. He stood next to the table, and Brittany stood beside him. She gazed at him with that same adoring look Beth had seen on the girl's face that day at the Dairy Dream.

Max put an arm around her, and she leaned closer to him. Beth's heart twisted. She wanted to run to her son and tell him to stay away from the girl. Any girl. But she knew she couldn't do that. How embarrassing would that be for Max? She released a shaky breath and forced herself to turn away.

Chapter Seven

Clay stood near the campfire as the flames gobbled the kindling and licked at the bigger logs. Smoke and sparks traveled heavenward. Logs for sitting formed a semicircle around the fire pit. He looked across the flames toward the tents. Beth emerged from hers. She had donned a royal-blue sweatshirt with gold lettering across the front. He couldn't read it from a distance, but the colors said Pinecrest High School. While she walked toward the campfire, she shrugged on a tan jacket over the sweatshirt. Silhouetted against the pastel-colored sky, she stopped and glanced around.

Watching her, he tried to figure out his attraction to her. She didn't seem to like him much. Why couldn't he get that message through his head? Every time she was around him, he couldn't miss the annoyed expression that lingered around her often forced smile. Hadn't he already told himself to stay away from her? His mission was to be a witness for the Lord and keep Max on the right track. Yet he couldn't deal with Max without dealing with Max's mother, right? Or was that just a convenient excuse to get involved in Beth's life as well?

Shoving the troublesome questions from his mind, he approached Sam. "Are you ready for the campfire?"

"Yeah. As soon as the cleanup is complete, we'll get everyone down here." Sam peered at Clay in the dim light. "Hey, great going on getting Max and Beth to come."

"Hopefully, we'll be seeing a lot more of Max. He told me he's going to start attending your youth programs."

"That's terrific news." Sam clapped Clay on the back. "How did this come about?"

"We had a talk the other night, and I strongly urged him to give it a try. We'll see what happens." Clay wished he could confide in Sam about what had occurred with Max, but it had to remain confidential. It had to remain a matter of prayer. "I'm hopeful that he'll follow through. He's the one who got Beth to come."

"Well, that's a good start." Sam nudged Clay. "Don't look now, but I think I know the real reason Max decided to come on the campout."

Clay turned slowly and followed Sam's gaze across the meadow. Max's height made him stand out, and Clay spotted the little redhead beside him. The one who had been with him on moving day. Had Max known she would be here? Her presence could explain his sudden change of mind.

Clay looked at Sam. "I don't remember her name."

"Brittany Gorman."

"That's right—Brittany. She came over to help the day Beth and Max moved. Does she usually come to church functions?" Clay asked. He hadn't seen her at the party after the game. Maybe she had attended the same party as Max.

"She came to a couple of things during the summer. Her family attends church sporadically. I'm glad to see them here this weekend. I hope it'll encourage more regular attendance." Sam glanced around the campground. "That's why I like these kinds of outings. They make folks feel more comfortable about going to church."

"You mean Max and Beth, too, right?"

Sam nodded. "Sure. Kim's been inviting Beth to church since they first met."

"Yeah, I heard she even used you as bait." Clay grinned.

"That's what I've been told. Now she's probably using you."

"She did mention that possibility, but I'm a lousy lure. The woman doesn't like me."

"What makes you say that?"

"Just trust me. I know." Clay smiled wryly. "I think the best way to get Beth interested in church is through Max. We need to convince her that he'll have good influences here."

"I'll make it a matter of prayer."

"Me, too."

"Hey, Pastor Sam, would you like to roast marshmallows with us?" One of the teenage girls held out a stick with a marshmallow on the end of it.

"Sure." Sam turned back to Clay. "We'll talk more later."

Clay watched Sam join the teenagers and younger children roasting marshmallows over the campfire. Beth stood off to one side watching, too. The firelight danced across her face and made her expression hard to read.

She appeared to be looking at Max. Laughing, he and Brittany fed each other marshmallows. What did Beth think about their pairing off?

Hoping to gain some insight, Clay continued to observe the interaction. He was still puzzled over Max's sudden turnaround concerning the campout.

Other folks began finding their way down to the fire from all corners of the campsite. Soon everyone was gathered together. Many of the teens sat on the logs, while the adults sat on lawn chairs at the back of the circle.

Standing on a makeshift stage at one end of the campfire, Sam greeted everyone. After announcing the next day's itinerary, including morning worship service, canoeing, hiking and numerous games, he said, "We have a real treat tonight. It's talent night. And we have lots of talent here. Let's bring up our emcee for the evening, Brian Petit."

Applause greeted Brian as he made his way to the platform. He picked up the microphone run from a cord to one of the nearby RVs. He greeted everyone and ran down the evening's agenda. He announced the first performance, a group of middle-school students who put on a skit illustrating the Bible story of the talents. Following the skit, several soloists sang, and then a small children's choir performed. Several women did a humorous skit about raising children. One of the men in the group got up and did a comedy routine that emphasized putting trust in God. He had the group laughing so hard, some people had tears streaming down their cheeks. A singing group ended the talent program. Brian asked all the performers to stand for another round of applause. When the clapping subsided, he reintroduced Sam.

Sam came back to the stage and took the microphone. "I'm going to read some Scripture, and then Clay Reynolds is going to give us a testimony."

Clay smiled as heads turned his way. When Sam opened his Bible, Clay prayed silently. *Lord, give me the words that will touch some hearts here tonight. Especially Max and Beth.*

Clay listened as Sam spoke. "I'm going to read from Romans twelve, verses four through eight.

"'Just as each of us has one body with many members, and these members do not all have the same function, so in Christ we who are many form one body, and each member belongs to all the others. We have different gifts, according to the grace given us. If a man's gift is prophesying, let him use it in proportion to his faith. If it is serving, let him serve; if it is teaching, let him teach; if it is encouraging, let him encourage; if it is contributing to the needs of others, let him give generously; if it is leadership, let him govern diligently; if it is showing mercy, let him do it cheerfully.'"

Sam motioned for Clay to come up onstage.

Clay took the microphone. "Thanks, Sam, for inviting me to share my story tonight. And thanks to all who shared their talents. That's kind of the topic of my testimony. It took me many years to let God use my talents for Him. I'm hoping what I say tonight will help you start using your talents now and not waste as much time as I did."

Clay stepped off the stage and drew closer to the

audience. The faces of the crowd glowed in the firelight. He had their rapt attention, even the younger children waited to hear what he had to say. "Like the Scripture says, God has given us all different gifts or talents. The first thing you need to do is find out what that gift is. Then use it for God's glory. Sometimes we don't always realize what our talent is. You might try something and find out you aren't very good at that particular thing. That's okay. If any of you sit near me during a hymn, you'll soon find out my talent isn't singing."

The audience chuckled.

"I found out early in life that I had a pretty good mind and what my mother called the 'gift of gab.' But I wasn't interested in using it for God. In fact, I wasn't interested in God at all." Clay opened his Bible. "I was interested in my own pleasure, like it says here in Galatians six, verses seven and eight. 'Do not be deceived: God cannot be mocked. A man reaps what he sows. The one who sows to please his sinful nature, from that nature will reap destruction; the one who sows to please the Spirit, from the Spirit will reap eternal life.' I was reaping a lot of destruction in my life."

Clay looked up and scanned the audience. His gaze briefly touched on Max and then Beth. Max didn't look away, but Beth did. What did that mean? Was she even willing to listen? "Pastor Sam is going to talk to the parents tomorrow morning. So I'm especially talking to the young people tonight. I hope you can learn from what I say and not make all the same stupid mistakes I made.

"I spent a lot of years in rebellion against God and my parents. I thought I knew better than anyone how to run my life. I was really just a selfish, spoiled kid who wanted what I wanted when I wanted it, no matter what anyone said or whoever got hurt."

Clay paused for a moment and looked over the crowd again. He met Max's gaze. Wondering whether he could get through to Max, Clay continued. "I partied through high school and much of college. I still managed to finish college and get a law degree, but I wasn't very happy. Somehow I thought being a lawyer for nonprofit organizations would fulfill the emptiness in my life, because I thought I was doing something worthwhile. I was helping people, wasn't I? But for some reason there was no satisfaction in it. Then I met a young woman, someone you all know, Jillian Rodgers Lawson. She showed me what it meant to really serve God when I helped her set up her charitable foundation. She had an amazing talent for giving, and she challenged me to use *my* talents for God, as it says in the verses from Romans that Sam read. I've been trying to do that ever since. And now I want to encourage you to find *your* talent. Whether it's something in the limelight or something in the background, God can use everyone. Let God use you."

Clay stepped back onto the stage. Sam followed and closed the evening's events with a prayer. Afterward several of the teens came up to Clay and thanked him for his testimony. Max wasn't among them.

While Clay helped put away the sound equipment, he wondered about Max's presence at the campout. Was he just going through the motions to keep Clay from telling Beth about Friday night? Then, of course, there was the Brittany aspect of the weekend. How should he handle that, if at all? Was any of this really his business?

With questions cluttering his mind, Clay stood near

the extinguished campfire. Flashlights hovered in the darkness as folks slowly made their way to their tents or campers. A quarter moon, dancing above the treetops, bathed the meadow in a soft light. Stars dotted the darkness. Clay searched for Beth, but he didn't see her. What had she thought of his testimony? He wanted so much to convince her that, no matter what she had done in the past, God could use her now. But maybe she didn't want that.

Clay guessed that he and Beth shared a common history of rebellion against parents and God. Could he ever get her to share about hers? He had somehow hoped that hearing about his wild, troubled youth tonight might make her realize that she, too, could come back to God. That God was waiting with open arms to welcome her. Maybe she needed more time.

As he made his way to his tent, the beam of his flashlight lit the ground ahead of him. Scattered around the camp, tents looked like giant luminarias as people settled in for the night. When he neared his, the light from Beth's tent went out. Shining the flashlight on his own tent a few yards away, he saw two figures standing close together in front of it. As quickly as the light hit them, they sprang apart.

Max and Brittany.

"Hi, there," Clay said as he stopped in front of them. "Saying good night?"

Brittany nodded. "Yeah. I was just going. See you tomorrow, Max, Mr. Reynolds."

"Sure, Brittany. Good night." Max squeezed her hand and watched her leave before turning to Clay. "We weren't doing anything."

"Did I say you were?"

"No, but it was the way you looked at us."

"And how was that?"

"Like you didn't approve."

"That thought is coming from somewhere other than me." Clay raised his eyebrows. "Maybe you've got a guilty conscience?"

"Not me."

"Well, good. Then there should be no problem." Clay opened the tent flap. "I'm going to call it a night. What about you?"

"Might as well." Max scowled. "Just 'cause we have to share a tent doesn't mean I have to talk to you."

Clay smiled. "You seem to be assuming a lot about me. First, that I disapprove of you and Brittany. Second, that you have to talk to me."

Sighing, Max lowered his gaze and kicked at a clump of grass. "I thought that's why you were sharing a tent with me. So you could…" His voiced trailed off.

"Could what?"

"Oh, I don't know." Max looked up. "I thought after this morning you were going to get me out here and give me a lecture."

"I said what I had to say last night. The rest is up to you. You do what you promised, we have a deal. Otherwise, you know the consequences."

"You'll tell my mom about the other night?"

"Yeah. So, we still have a deal?"

Max didn't say anything. He looked past Clay, then finally met his gaze. "Yeah. We have a deal."

"And, Max. As far as the talking goes. If you decide you want to talk to someone, I'm available."

Without another word Max went into the tent. Clay stared after him. Everything in him wanted to take the kid and shake some sense into him. Tell him to wise up and get the chip off his shoulder. But Clay forced himself to wait outside the tent to avoid the temptation. Max had agreed to their deal. That should be enough for now. Giving unwanted advice at this point would accomplish nothing.

Lord, I pray that You will give me the opportunity to talk with Max. Soften his heart. Let him listen to Your word. Please give me the wisdom to say the right things at the right time.

With that prayer firmly in mind, Clay entered the tent. Max was already in his sleeping bag with his back turned. Clay read that as a Do Not Disturb sign. Max didn't want any conversation tonight.

The cool morning air greeted Beth as she stepped from her tent. She snuggled into a gray hoodie with her college emblem on the front. The sun shone brightly just above the trees. She looked at the nearby tent. Was Max up? If she went to find out, she might run into Clay. She didn't want to deal with him so early in the morning.

Oh, what was she worried about? During the campfire session he hadn't talked to her. Even afterwards, he didn't bother to talk with her. Somehow she had expected him to seek her out as he had done so many times before. She should have been glad he'd left her alone. Instead, a flicker of disappointment nagged at her.

What did she want? For him to bug her about changing her life as he had changed his? When he started talking last night, she hadn't wanted to look at him, because she was sure he was talking right to her. But maybe that was only in her mind. What, if anything, would happen today?

"Hey, Mom."

Beth turned as Max trotted toward her. "Hi. Did you sleep all right?"

"Yeah. This camping stuff isn't so bad." He grinned. "How about you?"

"It was okay. Can't say it's something I want to do on a regular basis. You ready for breakfast?"

"Sure."

Falling into step with Max, she saw that the chow line had already formed. The smell of bacon and eggs filled the air as they drew near the camp stoves. They joined the crowd.

Beth took a plate and moved through the line. When she saw Kim, who was dishing out scrambled eggs, Beth asked, "Was I supposed to be helping with breakfast?"

"Oh, no. The meal crews were decided weeks ago when we planned the weekend." Smiling, Kim put a large spoonful of eggs on Beth's plate. "See you later at the worship service."

"Yeah," Beth replied. The worship service. How was she going to get through that? She hadn't been to church in a long time. She hadn't listened to a real sermon in years. Would the preaching make her feel unworthy? Hopeless? She tried not to think about it.

While Beth's mind buzzed with questions, Brittany approached the line. "Hi, Mrs. Carlson."

"Hi, Brittany."

"Hey, Max." The redhead smiled shyly at him. "A bunch of us are sitting over there."

"Hey, Brittany." Max looked to where she pointed, then back at Beth. "I'm going to sit with the other kids. Okay, Mom?"

"Sure." Beth watched him lope away with Brittany by his side. Max was a year younger than Brittany Gorman and her friends. Could hanging out with older kids create problems for Max?

Trying to put the troubling thought aside, she looked for a place to eat. Kim was working, and Beth hated to sit with strangers. Then she spied Lori Gorman. Should she sit with Brittany's mother?

Taking a deep breath, Beth marched over to the table before she could change her mind. "Mind if I sit here?"

Glancing up, Lori smiled. "Hi, Beth. We'd love to have you join us. Let me introduce you to my husband, Dave."

Beth shook hands with Dave. Then Lori proceeded to introduce her to everyone else at the table. After the introductions, Beth quickly started eating so she wouldn't have to engage in small talk. She could listen while the others talked.

But then Lori turned her way. "How about you, Beth? Are you planning to attend the parenting classes being offered at the church?"

Parenting classes? She must have missed that part of the conversation. Didn't Lori know Beth wasn't a member of the church? "I haven't heard anything about them." Beth wondered why Kim hadn't mentioned them. She was *always* trying to involve Beth in church activities.

"The classes start in a couple of weeks on Thursday evenings."

Shaking her head, Beth knew why Kim hadn't said anything. "I can't. I take classes in Spokane on Thursday nights."

"Oh, that's too bad. I'm really looking forward to learning some new tips. Raising children, especially teenagers, is so hard these days. We need all the help we can get."

"Yeah," Beth agreed, knowing she was forever struggling with parenting questions of her own.

"Do you have any children other than Max?"

"No. How about you?"

"Brittany's our oldest. We also have two boys, twelve and fourteen."

"How long have you lived in Pinecrest?"

"A little over a year. Dave works in Spokane, but we liked the idea of small-town living, so we bought a house out here."

"Pinecrest is a nice little town." Beth began to realize it was easy to talk with Lori.

"So far we like it. We decided we should get involved in a church again, so we came on this campout to get acquainted."

Church. Something Beth didn't want to discuss. So much for the easy conversation. What would Lori say if she knew Beth's feelings on the subject? She didn't want to find out. Finishing her last bite of food, she glanced around, seeking an excuse to leave. "Kim could use some help over there, so I'm going to give her a hand. It was nice talking to you."

"Sure," Lori said with a smile. "See you later."

Beth hurried off. She joined Kim, who was just closing a bag of trash.

"Hey, Kim, got room for this?" Beth held out her paper plate and cup.

"Yeah. Put 'em right in here." Kim opened up the trash bag and then closed it again. "Are you ready to head down to the worship service? We can dump this on the way."

Her stomach churning, Beth nodded. "Okay."

"Great. We can stop by our tent. I'll get my Bible, and we can grab a couple of chairs."

"Where's Brian?"

"I suspect he'll come strolling in just as the singing starts. He went fishing with Sam and Clay early this morning. They're planning a big fish fry."

Helping Kim with the trash, Beth remembered last year when Max had gone on a campout with the church teens. He had been so proud when he brought home the fish he caught. Would he go fishing during this campout, or was he too wrapped up with Brittany? He wasn't that same little boy, who had been like an overgrown puppy. Eager to please. He had grown and changed so much in the past year that Beth felt as though she hardly knew him anymore. He was growing up way too fast.

While Beth waited outside Kim's tent, she almost wished she could attend the parenting classes. Of course then she would be expected to attend other things at church. All her old feelings of inadequacy inundated her when she thought about the last church where her father had ministered.

She had seen her mother try so hard to please the people in the congregation, but someone always had a complaint. People who were supposed to be Christians did so much damage to others with their constant criticism. How was that following God?

Her father had seemed above it all, but maybe he had felt the pressure, too. Maybe that's why he had changed churches so often. Maybe that's why he had expected so much of Beth.

And, in her rebellion, she had let him down.

Now she was here, on the periphery of this church. These people seemed so different from the congregations of her youth. But could she trust them to accept her and her faults?

"You look deep in thought." Kim's voice brought Beth out of her musings.

Smiling, she shrugged. "Guess I have a lot on my mind."

"Anything to do with a certain handsome neighbor of yours?"

Beth frowned. "No. I was thinking about Max and how fast he's growing up. I'm not ready for that."

Kim came over and put an arm around Beth's shoulders. "I'm sorry I keep teasing you about Clay. You have my permission to yell at me the next time I do that."

"I don't want to yell at you. Maybe if I pull on my earlobe or something when you go into matchmaker mode, you can break the habit."

Kim laughed. "I love having you for a friend."

"Me, too." Beth's heart felt lighter as she and Kim found a spot for their lawn chairs among those gathered for morning worship.

While Beth waited for the service to begin, she scanned the crowd for Max. He sat up front with the teen contingent. Brittany wasn't with him. Why not? Then she saw the reason. Brittany sat with her parents and two brothers.

Beth leaned over to Kim. "I thought Sam had to speak, and those guys aren't back yet."

"Worried about Clay?" Kim whispered as she gave Beth one of the song sheets being passed down the row.

Beth immediately pulled on one earlobe.

Grimacing, Kim mouthed the word *sorry*.

Before Beth could comment, Brian slipped his chair in beside Kim's. He gave his wife a quick peck on the cheek. Beth glanced at the stage, where the song leader had begun the first song. With a Bible in his hand, Sam, still in his fishing gear, stood off to one side. While she was looking at the stage, Clay managed to get his chair next to hers. She turned to look at him.

He leaned closer and grinned. "Looks like we got here just under the wire."

Nodding, Beth refused to think about what his presence was doing to her pulse rate. Instead, she buried her face in the song sheet and belted out the hymn, something she hadn't done in years. And beside her, Clay sang off-key. He hadn't been kidding when he said his talent wasn't singing. She tried not to smile at his less-than-stellar vocalization. Somehow the off-key performance touched her heart and made Clay seem less intimidating. He didn't let the fact that he couldn't sing bother him. He sang anyway.

After the song ended, he leaned close again. "You have a nice voice."

"Thanks," she whispered. Could he really know she had a nice voice when he couldn't carry a tune?

While one of the men said an opening prayer, Beth gave herself a mental shake. *Take Clay's compliment at face value instead of trying to dissect it.* For too long she had put herself down. Reasons for her low self-esteem had piled up over the years. She had let herself feel second-rate because she had a GED rather than a regular high school diploma. Because she was an unwed mother. Because she was an aide instead of a teacher. Being around people like Clay, who had a law degree, made her feel even more inadequate. She needed to remind herself that next spring she would be a college graduate. She needed to remember that she had accomplished a lot. Most important, she was raising a fine young man.

When the next song started, Clay's tone-deaf rendition of the tune rang out with gusto. His unabashed enthusiasm reminded her of the Scripture her father used to quote from the Psalms. *Make a joyful noise unto the Lord.* Clay certainly knew how to do that.

Beth sang the words, but Clay meant them. Did she dare think about God being there for her? No. She couldn't let herself. She would only come up short. She would never be good enough.

But wasn't that what Clay had talked about during his testimony? That God didn't give up on anyone. That He wanted everyone. No matter how far they had strayed. She wanted to believe that message, but she feared taking that step. Negatives from the past heightened her wariness when it came to God.

Still, she settled in to listen to Sam's message.

Sam stepped to the microphone and opened his Bible. "The Lord told us to go fishing for people, so I thought I'd dress for the part. You'll have to put up with me this morning since Pastor Craig is preaching to the folks who remained in town for worship."

The crowd chuckled before Sam continued. "I'd like

to read from the hundred and twenty-seventh Psalm. The first verse. 'Unless the Lord builds the house, its builders labor in vain.'" Sam looked out at the audience. "Even though you have a Christian home, it doesn't mean you won't have problems."

That was an understatement. Sam's words reminded Beth of her childhood and the problems her family had encountered, many of them because of her. She wanted to put her hands over her ears, but she resisted the childish impulse. She didn't want to sit here and listen to another sermon, another lecture on how she had messed up her life. But Sam's next words caught her attention.

"Talk to your children. Find out how they feel about your family. You might not like what you hear, but it's a starting point for evaluation. And don't let the evaluation lead you to guilt. Guilt alone will accomplish nothing. If there are problems, there has to be change. Let that change begin with you. What kind of example have you been lately?"

Sam's words hit Beth hard, but not in the way she had expected. She had thought his sermon would dredge up the old guilt about her past. Instead, they made her look at the present and her relationship with Max in a new and hopeful light.

In the past year he had seemed to grow up and away from her. Some of that was natural for a teenage boy. But in the process she had let communication between them drift. They didn't talk the way they once had. And now, with Brittany in the picture, talking with Max might become more important than ever. If she were honest with herself, had she let work and school take priority over spending time with Max? Was that partly why they didn't talk as much anymore?

What could she do to make it different? She didn't want to feel guilty for trying to better herself by getting a college degree. Ultimately, that would benefit both her and Max.

During the rest of the sermon Beth thought about the kind of rapport she had with her son. What kind of response would he give if she asked him how he felt about his home life? How did he feel about never having had a father in his life? Had she been a good parent? Or had she been just as bad with Max as she felt her parents had been with her? Too many questions. No answers. Yet. But she felt energized about reviewing her relationship with her son.

When Sam ended his sermon, he stepped off the stage and the song leader began the final song. People stood, and Beth saw the Gormans approach Sam. He talked with them privately while the congregation finished singing the song.

Then Sam turned to the audience. "Dave and Lori Gorman and their three children, Brittany, Andrew and Sean, have decided they want to put God first in their family." Sam handed the microphone to Dave.

"We want to thank this congregation for making us feel welcome even though our attendance at church has been infrequent. We want to change that. Pastor Sam's message has made us realize how important it is to keep God at the center of our family. Lori and I plan to attend his parenting classes and invite some friends to attend as well." Dave handed the microphone back to Sam.

"Let's have a prayer for the Gormans." Sam bowed his head.

Beth gazed at her feet. She didn't want to think about God. That would mean examining her life more than she already had. Today she felt pulled in by God's call. His presence somehow seemed real for the first time since she'd been a teen in crisis, devastated and disillusioned by the way some so-called Christians had treated her. She still couldn't quite throw aside all her old doubts, and she wasn't sure God could forgive her for turning her back on Him for all these years. Clay seemed to think so. And he seemed certain that a relationship with God and a church family would benefit both her and Max. Could he be right?

Sam ended his prayer, and people filed forward to greet the Gormans. Beth hung back. She wasn't really a part of this church. She was an outsider. She didn't belong. How was this weekend affecting Max? She was only here because of him.

Max.

She looked around for him. She spotted him standing near the front with a group of teens who were talking enthusiastically with Brittany and her brothers. What might her family's commitment mean to Max? Would he want his own little family to make a similar commitment? Beth sighed. Would she be up to all the challenges ahead?

Chapter Eight

Clay doused the last embers of the campfire with a bucket of water. A hissing noise accompanied the smoke that rose from the darkened embers. He shoveled dirt onto the coals to make sure they wouldn't fire back to life.

That's the way he wished he could bury the feelings he had for Beth. The campfire was dead and gone, but his affection for Max's mom grew with every hour he spent in her presence. But her determination to avoid him seemed just as strong as his wish to be near her. Somehow his head had gotten the message, but his heart didn't have a clue.

Still, the campout had brought Beth out of her shell, and he had enjoyed every minute of seeing her sing, gab and play volleyball with the others. She had helped Kim organize activities for the younger children so their parents could go hiking and canoeing. When the parents returned Beth had the children's attention as she told them stories. She had him spellbound as well.

And then there was Max, who was just as bright—

and stubborn—as his mother. Would Max make the right decisions for his future? Now that the weekend was over, would Max voluntarily join in the youth group's activities, or would his participation hinge on not having his mother find out about the drunken party he'd attended? And how would Beth view things? She had let Max attend the campout, but would she encourage him to take part in the other activities when she had little use for church herself?

Clay wished he could gather all the church teens together and tell them to keep Max busy and out of trouble, but that wouldn't work. Clay just had to pray that would happen. Not that churchgoing kids always did everything right, but from Clay's observation, they helped one another stay on track most of the time. They cared about God and each other. Max could benefit from hanging out with them rather than with kids who drank and partied all the time. Throwing the final shovelful of dirt onto the fire pit, Clay sent up a prayer for Max.

With shovel in hand, Clay strolled across the meadow. Folks were packing up the last of their gear. The moon peeked over the mountain ridge visible between two tall pines silhouetted against the pale light. Clay stopped and took in the handiwork of God's creation. Surely God, who could create such beauty, could help one confused teenage boy.

As Clay put the shovel in the church van he'd be driving back, Sam and several young men from the youth group approached, carrying the now-empty coolers.

"What do you want us to do with these?" Sam asked.

"Put them in here." Clay opened the back of the van.

"After you do that, I'd appreciate it if you'd get the grills, too."

"Sure," the boys chorused.

After the kids left, Sam turned to Clay. "I need a favor. I promised the kids that we'd stop for ice cream on the way home, but I can't hang around to take them. Would you do it?"

"Hey, no problem."

"Thanks. I'm headed home," Sam said with a wave.

While Sam jogged away and got into his truck, Clay spotted Beth loading things into Brian's SUV. Clay headed that way with an idea about how to get a few answers to some of his questions about Max.

"Hey, Beth."

She turned, her expression obscured in the dim light. "What?"

"Is it okay if Max goes home with me?"

For a moment she said nothing. Then she shook her head. "No. Absolutely not."

Frowning, Clay puzzled at the panic in her voice. "Why? We're just stopping for ice cream."

"I don't care. I won't have my son riding on the back of that motorcycle."

He touched her arm. "Beth, do you see a motorcycle?"

She scanned the area. Shaking her head, she returned her gaze to his. "No."

"I didn't come up on my bike. I'm driving one of the church vans back to town, and I just wanted to know whether it was okay for Max to come with a bunch of the kids to get ice cream on the way home."

"Oh." She seemed embarrassed at her outburst. "All right. He can go if he wants."

"Where is he?"

"He's helping put the canoes into the storage barn."

"Thanks. I'll ask him." Jogging away, Clay wondered why Beth was so automatically distrustful of him. And she sure hated motorcycles. That had been quite evident the day her car broke down.

Clay saw Max as the group finished putting away the canoes. He stepped up to Max. "Did you enjoy the weekend?"

Max gave Clay a wary look. Like mother, like son. "It was okay."

"Good." Clay decided not to comment on the rather noncommittal response. "A bunch of the kids are riding back with me. We're stopping for ice cream. You wanna come with us?"

Max shrugged. "I'd have to ask my mom first."

"I already did. She said it's up to you."

"I don't know. I'll think about it."

"Okay. We'll be leaving as soon as the campgrounds are clean." Clay watched as Max wandered over to where his mom was helping Brian and Kim. Despite the boy's belligerent talk on Saturday morning, Clay suspected Max didn't want to displease his mother. Her opinion counted a lot to him. Clay just hoped that her opinion about church wouldn't dissuade Max from participating in its youth activities.

One by one the cars, campers and vans left the campsite as folks headed home. A stream of red taillights trailed down the access road. The quarter moon sliced its way through the night as it climbed higher in the darkened sky. Carrying flashlights, Clay and Brian made one last round of the camp to make sure everything was in order.

"Are you stopping for ice cream?" Clay asked as they approached Brian's SUV.

"No. We've got to get home. Beth said she needed to get back, too. She said Max is riding with you. Right?"

"Yeah. We're ready to head out."

Minutes later the church van followed the SUV out of the camp. The laughter and lively conversation of a dozen teenagers filled the van as Clay headed toward Pinecrest. He scanned the group in the rearview mirror. Although Max sat next to Brittany, the two young people weren't paying much attention to each other. They were involved in conversation with the other teens. Good. Since Brittany's family had renewed their commitment to God, would she have a positive influence on Max's relationship to the church? Or might he sway her from her commitment?

Prayer was the only answer. *Lord, please give Brittany the strength to stand for You and Your principles in her relationship with Max.*

Whenever Clay thought about Max, thoughts of Max's mom were never far behind. How should he deal with his feelings for Beth? He reminded himself that, whatever his feelings, she obviously didn't share them. She still looked at him with distrust. Maybe that was just as well. Too many barriers stood between them. They didn't seem to want the same things from life. He wanted to serve God. She didn't. She liked living in a small town. He didn't. About the only thing they shared was a concern for Max. And maybe it should stay that way for the good of them all.

The van headlights illuminating the highway ahead reminded Clay that he should keep his attention focused on the Lord. He couldn't let a pair of blue eyes sidetrack him from what he knew was right. He only intended to stay in Pinecrest for a short time. Getting involved with Beth wouldn't be fair to either of them.

Clay arrived in Pinecrest and drove to the Dairy Dream. Once he stopped, the teens spilled from the van and rushed to the two windows to place their orders. Soon they were sitting at the picnic tables at the back of the building. The laughter and talk continued while they ate their ice cream. Clay joined in, but something was missing. Despite his earlier thoughts concerning Beth, he couldn't help wishing she were here, too.

After the kids finished their cones, they piled back into the van. Much to Clay's surprise, Max claimed the front seat while Brittany sat in the back again. Clay dropped each kid off at home. Finally, only he and Max were left riding through the quiet streets. Max was equally quiet as Clay parked the van in front of their house.

Reaching for the door handle, Max glanced back at Clay. "What did you do with your bike?"

"It's in the storage shed at the church. I'll pick it up in the morning."

"Why didn't you pick it up before you came home?"

"What was I going to do with you?"

"I could've ridden on the back."

"Not if I wanted to live to tell about it. Your mother nearly took my head off when she thought I was going to take you home on that bike."

"She did?"

"Yeah." Clay looked closely at Max. "Any reason for that?"

Max didn't say anything. He just stared straight ahead. The streetlight sent a beam across the boy's solemn expression. Finally he spoke. "She doesn't like motorcycles."

"I got that part. Do you know why?"

Still not looking at Clay, Max nodded. "She told me my dad was killed in a motorcycle accident."

"Oh, wow. That's tough. I'm sorry. No wonder she doesn't like bikes. When did that happen?"

"Before I was born."

"So you never knew your dad."

Finally looking at Clay, Max shook his head. "About all I know is that my mom and him weren't married, and she doesn't like to talk about it."

"Does that bother you?"

"It used to, but I think talking about it makes her sad. And I don't want that."

"Then why did you get drunk the other night? You knew *that* would upset your mom, didn't you?"

Max turned away. "Do we have to talk about that?"

"Not necessarily. But I'd like for you to tell me what's going on with you." Clay drummed his fingers on the steering wheel.

"Like what?"

"First, why you changed your mind about the campout just like that." Clay snapped his fingers.

"You wouldn't understand."

"Try me."

"You made me mad." Max balled his hands into

fists. "You act like you can run my life just because I messed up once."

"I'm not trying to run your life."

"Seems that way to me. Telling me I have to go to all that church stuff or you'll tell Mom about that night."

"I'm only trying to help you make some tough decisions."

"I can make my own decisions."

"Like the decision you made the other night?"

"That was one bad choice. No need to put me in prison for life." Max frowned. "I went to the campout so you wouldn't tell my mom. Like I said, I don't want to make her sad."

"So what do you intend to do now?"

"I'll do what you said about the church stuff." Max grimaced.

"Is that going to be so bad? What about Brittany?"

"Leave her out of it. This has nothing to do with her. This is about my mom."

"So you're not just going to the youth activities to be with Brittany?"

Max glared at Clay. "Do I have a choice? You said if I didn't go, you'd tell my mom I got drunk. Well, I don't want that to happen. Brittany or no Brittany. Besides, we're just friends."

"Okay. I get the picture. Let's call it a night."

"Sure." Max hopped out of the van and sprinted to the house almost as if he thought Clay might come after him and grill him with more questions.

Sitting in the van, Clay thought about Max. As the boy had said, Brittany or no Brittany, hopefully with the threat of his mom's finding out about the drunken party hanging over his head, Max wouldn't venture too far off the straight and narrow again anytime soon. But only time would tell.

Clay stared at the white two-story house, his temporary home. Temporary. That's the way he liked it, right? At least that's what he kept telling himself. But his life was becoming more and more involved with Max and Beth. They had insinuated themselves into his every waking thought. When it came time to go, how would he feel about leaving them behind?

Squinting against the bright September afternoon sun, Beth stood near the Dunk the Hunk booth as Clay and Sam walked toward her. "I thought you guys had backed out on me. One of you is on in five minutes. Who's going first?"

Clay and Sam looked at each other. "He is," they chorused.

"You have four minutes to decide," Beth said, barely able to keep from staring at Clay, who was clad in shorts and a tank top that showed off lots of gorgeous muscles. Sunglasses covered his eyes, making him look even more dangerously handsome.

Beth quickly looked at Sam and hoped Clay didn't realize how much his presence disturbed her. "Did you guys bring a change of clothes?"

Sam nodded. "Yeah, we left them in my car."

"Okay." Beth glanced at her watch. "Time for a new victim. Which one of you will it be?"

"I think youth should go first." Sam grinned at Clay.

Clay laughed. "Okay, old man, but your turn's coming."

Sam slapped Clay on the back. "I've got my throwing arm ready."

"You won't do any throwing unless you purchase tickets." Beth tried to gather her wits and ignore the way Clay looked with his ponytail grazing his bare shoulders.

"Where do I buy the tickets?" Sam asked.

Beth pointed to the stand near the front of the school. "Right over there. I've got towels for you to dry off with when you get out." She reached behind the booth, brought out two towels and handed one to Clay.

Removing his sunglasses, he draped the towel on one rung of the ladder. His gray eyes twinkled with mischief. "You think I'm going to get wet?"

"You can count on it." She couldn't help looking into those laughing eyes. They seemed to say to her, *Lighten up and have some fun.* But she couldn't let down her guard enough to have fun around Clay. She might find herself liking him too much. But if she didn't look him in the eye, she would probably stare at his muscled chest. Where should she look? She shouldn't look at him, period.

Beth marched over to Sam and took his ticket. "I'll hold your towel until it's your turn."

"Thanks." Sam taunted Clay from the sidelines while he took his seat in the dunking booth. "She's right. You won't be dry for long."

"Remember you're in here after me," Clay called out to Sam.

"I'm not worried. You throw like a girl." Grinning, Sam made a practice pitching motion. "I'm ready. Be prepared to get wet." He took one of the three balls Beth held out for him. He let the first pitch fly. The ball flew past the target and landed with a thud on the backdrop, then rolled harmlessly away from the tank.

"Looks like I'm not the only one who throws like a girl!" Clay yelled.

"Don't get too smug. I've still got two more chances." Sam loosened his arm with another exaggerated practice throw. Then he threw the second ball. It grazed the target before falling to the ground. "Hey, I hit the target, and he didn't go down."

Beth handed Sam the third ball. "You have to hit right on the bull's-eye, or it doesn't trigger the mechanism."

"Yeah. You've got to do it right!" Clay shouted. "This is your last chance, big fella. Don't blow it. You—"

Clay's last words drowned in the water. He came sputtering to the surface amid cheers and jeers from the crowd gathered to watch the sparring match between the two men.

"Think maybe you let yourself get too confident?" Sam grinned and glanced around. "Hey, Jillian, you want to try knocking Clay off his seat?"

"Sure." She handed her ticket to Beth. Taking her first ball, Jillian smiled. "Are you ready, Clay?"

"Yeah. Give it your best shot."

All three of Jillian's throws missed the target. "Don't say I never did you any favors, Clay."

A young boy stepped up and gave his ticket to Beth. She handed him the balls. He also failed to hit the target.

"Beth, you should take a turn," Jillian said after Beth retrieved the balls for the next person and put them on the stand.

"I'm working. I can't take a turn." Beth shook her head.

"Come on, Mom," Max called as he loped across the schoolyard toward the group. He stopped next to Beth and put an arm around her shoulders. "Take a turn."

"You take a turn." Beth ducked away from Max. "Besides, I don't have a ticket."

"Here's one." Kim joined the group. "I'd love to see you put Clay in the tank."

Jillian took Kim's ticket and waved it in the air. "I'll do your job while you take a turn, Beth."

Fuming inside, Beth shook her head. They were matchmaking again. She grabbed a ball. All right. She'd show them.

She stepped up to the mark. "He is getting too dry, isn't he?"

Beth forced herself to smile at Clay. Her heart beat faster. He smiled in return as if he knew she was having a hard time focusing on the target.

"Another futile attempt to knock me down. You should've saved your money, Beth." Clay laughed.

"It's for a good cause. Besides, I'm using Kim's ticket." Beth rolled the ball between her palms. The feel of it in her hands took her back years to the times when she had played softball with the neighborhood boys. She had been pretty good back then. What were the chances that she could throw that way now? "Since you're so sure I can't hit the target, you wanna put more on the line than my knocking you off your perch?"

"That depends on what it is."

"How about if I hit the target, you have to cut your hair?"

Grabbing his ponytail, he shook his head. "Can't do that. No way."

"If I'm going to miss, what do you have to worry about?" She tossed the ball into the air and caught it. Gaining a newfound confidence, she looked back at him and grinned. For some reason while he sat in that contraption, he didn't seem quite so intimidating. "Well, what do you say?"

"This hair is committed to a good cause. So I can't chance putting it on the line just in case you should get lucky." He grinned. "Besides, if you don't hurry and throw that ball, my time will be up. At quarter till the hour, I'm out of here."

"What's the good cause?"

"When my hair gets long enough, I donate it to an organization that makes wigs for children with cancer."

Beth took in that information with a growing respect for a man she was trying hard not to like. Why did he have to be so nice? So good-looking? So giving? She was annoyed with herself for asking those questions almost every time she encountered him. "If you're giving your hair away, why can't you cut it?"

"It has to be longer first. I figure about six more weeks till it's long enough."

"I've got a great idea!" Kim yelled from the sidelines. "If Beth dunks you, she gets to cut your hair when it's time. How about it, Clay?"

"Fine with me. Beth, you're wasting time. I'll be done before you throw the first ball." He held up his left arm as if to look at an imaginary watch. "And what do I get if you miss?"

Beth gripped the ball tighter. Now she would look bad if she didn't agree. Why couldn't Kim stay out of this? "That won't happen. But just to satisfy you, if I miss, I'll cook dinner for you every night next week."

"That sounds good. I can taste the home cooking now."

"Don't salivate too much. You're gonna get wet,

Clay." Beth heaved the ball toward the target. It hit the metal center with a clang, and Clay went into the water, making a big splash. The crowd cheered.

"Way to go, Mom!" Grinning from ear to ear, Max gave her a high five.

Clay came up wiping his face with his hands. "How'd you learn to throw like that?"

For the first time she had the upper hand. "Must've been an accident. And I have two more chances. So get back on your perch."

"Yes, ma'am," he said with a salute.

When Clay was back in position, Beth threw the ball. She hit the bull's-eye, and he went into the tank again. He sputtered to the surface. "You must be cheating or something."

"Nope. Do you remember my telling you how I used to play ball with the neighborhood boys? I guess I haven't lost my touch." Whistling, she tossed the ball from hand to hand while she waited for him to get back into place.

"You should take a turn in this thing," he said, settling in the seat.

"I don't qualify for Dunk the Hunk," she said, laughing. "And I have one more chance." She tossed the ball. It grazed the target but failed to knock him into the water.

"Well, what do you know? She missed, and my time's up." Clay climbed out of the booth and picked up his towel. "Your turn, Sam. Have fun."

Sam entered the dunking booth while a group gathered. They jostled for position, eager to see this popular teacher wind up in the water. Beth resumed her spot as ticket taker. Several of Sam's former students stood in line ready to try their hand at hitting the target that would send him splashing into the tank.

Beth tried to concentrate on her duties, but she had difficulty ignoring Clay. Still dripping, he stood nearby talking with Max while they waited in line to dunk the hunk. For some reason Max and Clay seemed to have become fast friends since the night of the first football game.

Maybe it was their common interest in football, but Beth worried about their connection. She liked Max's having an older male to consult about guy things. And she couldn't deny from what she had seen that Clay was a good role model. But would Max start looking at Clay in the context of having a father? Would Max push Clay at her in hopes of making that happen? She didn't want that.

Besides his pushing Clay at her, she worried about Max's pushing church at her. His sudden interest in church astounded her. He didn't just go occasionally as he had before but was there every time the youth group did something. In addition to the church stuff, Max now did all his chores without complaining, studied extra hard and spent hours working out for football. It was almost as if he had something to prove.

While Clay changed into his dry clothes, he thought about how Beth had dunked him. He had seen a glimpse of the woman who had so happily entertained the kids at the campout. He'd enjoyed watching her laugh today, even if it was at his expense. And, according to Kim, he would have another chance to see her in action during the kindergarten program.

Just before four o'clock Clay followed Sam, Jillian,

Kim and Brian into the gymnasium. Parents and grand-parents of the kindergarteners and friends of their families occupied the folding chairs set in rows on the gym floor near the stage. An upright piano sat in front of the closed red velvet curtain. Conversation buzzed while the audience waited.

At the top of the hour Beth, dressed in a mid-calf-length floral skirt and ribbed knit tunic, stepped around the curtain at the end of the stage near the piano. She had changed clothes, and she looked great. Clay couldn't help staring. He had to force himself to look away.

She stepped to the edge of the stage. "Mrs. Boyd couldn't be with us today because she's not feeling well, but the children are well prepared to present the story of the 'Bremen Town Musicians.'"

The audience applauded, and the curtain opened, re-vealing a chorus of children standing to one side on risers. A simple set, suitable for depicting the various scenes of the story, occupied center stage. Beth stood in front of the risers and directed the singing as the play began. The children's enthusiasm was evident from the gusto with which they said their lines and sang the songs. When the play ended, applause echoed through the gym as the children received a standing ovation.

Beth encouraged her charges to take their bows. The smiles on their faces told of their triumph. When the applause died down, a boy and a girl came from the wings and gave Beth a bouquet of flowers. She hugged each one and then thanked the audience for coming. After the curtain closed, people began filing out in search of their juvenile performers.

As parents collected their children, many stopped

to talk with Beth. Clay leaned against a wall near the door. Sam, Jillian, Kim and Brian had gone to the front to talk with Beth, but Clay hung back because he didn't want to face the reality of how much he cared about this woman. She was going to make an excellent teacher. He could tell by the way the children related to her. She brought joy to the kids and to their parents. He couldn't even begin to think of taking her away from this.

If he pursued his feelings for her, there would still come that day, all too soon, when he would leave Pinecrest. He wasn't going to stay here. And then there was the biggest obstacle of all. She didn't share his faith. These arguments went around and around in his head. Nothing had changed except that he was letting himself care more and more about her even as he tried to resist.

Finally Clay pushed himself away from the wall and headed to the front of the gym. Beth was still surrounded by well-wishers, children and parents. The setting suited her. She bubbled with enthusiasm. He liked seeing her this way. Why couldn't she act this way around him? But that would only make matters worse, wouldn't it?

"Hey, Clay, where have you been?" Brian waved Clay over.

"Just staying out of the way," Clay replied, not daring to look in Beth's direction.

"Well, Kim and Beth are about done here, and we're headed over to our house for the barbecue for the folks who worked on the festival. You coming?" Brian asked.

"Sitting in the dunking booth still counts as working on the festival?" Clay grinned.

"Absolutely." Kim turned to look at Beth. "Doesn't it, Beth?"

Beth nodded but didn't say anything. She immediately turned to talk with a group of children who were clamoring for her attention.

Kim turned back to Clay. "So we'll see you at our place?"

"Sure. I'll be over in a little while." Again Clay had the distinct impression that Beth didn't want him around. How could he change that? Then again, hadn't he told himself that was foolish thinking?

Chapter Nine

Brian and Kim's backyard buzzed with conversation as dozens of people gathered for the barbecue. Smoke curled from two grills sitting on the deck. Children ran through the yard in a game of tag. So much about this little town appealed to Clay—until he remembered how it was to live in a place like this where everyone knew everyone else's business. He didn't want that kind of life again.

While Clay stood watching all the activity, Kim came up to him. "Help yourself to something to drink. Lots of stuff in the coolers on the deck."

"I will in a minute." He glanced around the yard again and then back at Kim. "Are you people always having a party in this town?"

Kim laughed. "We do like to have fun. So we take advantage of any occasion that lends itself to a get-together. I kind of come by it naturally. My mom is the queen of the impromptu party. Ask my brother. When we were growing up, our house was the scene of many neighborhood and church functions. I loved it, but I'm not sure Sam did."

"Not sure Sam did what?" Jillian asked as she joined Kim and Clay.

"Enjoyed the chaos at our house when we were growing up. I was just telling Clay how Mom used to find any excuse to invite the church or neighbors over for a party."

"Sam did confide in me that sometimes it was over-whelming, but he finally got used it. And surprisingly enough he's kind of followed in her footsteps, even though he doesn't admit it."

"I think you helped him along in that direction," Kim said.

"So you don't mind knowing everyone in town and having everyone know you?" Clay looked from Jillian to Kim.

"No," they chorused.

Clay turned to Jillian. "And you like living here again after having moved away to the city?"

"Yeah." Jillian wrinkled her brow. "Why? Are you considering moving back to your hometown?"

"No. I just wondered how you felt about it." Clay didn't dare voice the idea that he might consider living in a small town like Pinecrest even if the idea kept niggling at the back of his mind. Especially every time he thought about Beth and Max.

"Well, the people I love are here. That made the difference for me." Jillian waved for Beth to join them. "Hey, Beth, come on over here."

With a less-than-enthusiastic smile, Beth made her way through the crowd to where they stood. "Hi."

"Here's our ace pitcher." Jillian laughed. "Sam is going to recruit you for the church softball team next spring now that he knows how well you pitch."

Beth shook her head. "I'm not going to have time for softball. I'll be busy studying."

"The softball league continues into the summer. You can play after you graduate." Jillian patted Beth on the back.

"We'll see," Beth replied.

"Beth, look." Kim nodded toward the other side of the yard. "Max and Brittany make such a cute couple. They remind me of Jillian and Sam when they were young."

"Did we look like that?" Jillian slipped her arm through Sam's as he joined the group.

"Yeah, you did look at me with that same unadulterated adoration." Sam chuckled.

"I think it was the other way around." Jillian gave him a playful push. "But I do think they're a cute couple."

"Well, I don't," Beth said, her expression somber.

Kim looked at Beth. "Why not?"

"Max is so young, and he's already got a lot on his plate. He doesn't need a girlfriend." Beth frowned.

Clay studied Beth's expression. She looked so unhappy. He wanted to ease her worry. "He told me they were just friends."

Beth bit her bottom lip. "I hope so. He's got plenty of time to be serious about girls. He doesn't need to start when he's fifteen."

"You've got a point." Sam nodded. "It's tough being a teenager these days. There's lots of pressure and temptations to overcome. And dating relationships are among them."

Beth looked across the yard at the teenagers. "I know. That's what I keep thinking about—" she hesitated "—what happened with Jillian's nephew, Dylan."

Sam patted Beth's shoulder. "I don't want to downplay your concerns, but hopefully the lessons I'm doing on abstinence with the youth group will help. I'm glad Max has been attending most of their activities."

"Did they help Dylan and Tori?" Beth replied, her chin jutting out.

"I wasn't teaching those lessons then. I had some guilt issues of my own to deal with. At the time I was afraid to teach something I hadn't practiced in my own life." Sam gazed at Beth. "I had to learn to forgive myself first."

Wide-eyed, she stared back. She started to open her mouth as if to say something, but then closed it. Before anyone else could comment, a loud whistle sounded across the yard. Brian clanged his grilling utensils together, and conversation ceased. He told everyone the food was ready. Then he said a prayer of thanks for the meal.

While Clay stood in line, he watched Beth, who stood on the other side of Sam and Jillian. Clay hadn't missed her shocked expression when Sam talked about his past. Would knowing about that help her realize how easily she could come back to God herself? Clay didn't miss the fact that she didn't want Max to repeat the mistakes of her youth. But she needed to know that forgiveness awaited her if only she would ask. How could he convey that message to her?

Lord, help Beth to see Your grace.

Beth balanced her plate and drink as she scanned the yard for a place to sit. Her stomach churned. Could she even eat? Had Sam said those things because he knew about her past? Why had she even thought no one would know? Anyone who knew her age could calculate that she had been sixteen when Max was born. What did she think she had been hiding?

Would the lessons Sam taught really keep Max from repeating her mistakes? She certainly hadn't been able to talk with her son about it. She had had the same guilt feelings that Sam had talked about. Could she find forgiveness as he had? The questions knotted her stomach even more.

After finding a chair under one of the shade trees in the yard, she balanced her plate on her lap. She stared at the food and wished life didn't have to be so complicated.

"Mind if I join you?"

Without waiting for her reply, Clay sat on the chair next to her. Beth glanced at him. "Be my guest."

"I just wanted to echo my agreement with Sam that we're glad Max is attending the youth functions at the church."

"I'm sure you are, since that's what you've wanted since you met him." She couldn't keep the sarcasm out of her voice.

"Is that a problem for you?"

She sighed. "I always said it was his decision. So if that's what he wants, I won't stand in his way."

"How about you? Can I convince you to come to church?"

Trying to avoid the question, Beth took a bite of her burger and chewed it with deliberate slowness. When would he tire of trying to get her to change her mind about church?

"We've got another church outing a few weeks from now. Adults only. How about that?" he asked, not waiting for her reply. "We've made reservations at one of the resorts up north. We're going to have a very relaxed retreat with some fun activities thrown in. A play at the Cutter Theatre in Metaline Falls and a train ride to see the fall foliage."

"Can't. I have class on Saturdays."

"Won't you be on your fall break?"

Now what could she say? She had no excuse. Just the truth. "That doesn't make any difference. I don't want to go."

"That's what you said about the campout. And you have to admit you had a good time, right?" His expression sent a you-can't-deny-it message.

Pressing her lips together, she shook her head. He had obviously taken the time to consider her college schedule. What did that mean? She almost wished it meant that he was interested in her on a romantic level, but that was silly, crazy thinking. She couldn't let herself be drawn in just to be let down. He was interested in getting her to church. She had to remind herself of that before she did something stupid and let herself care about him too much.

"So you'll go, right? I've even got a roommate for you," he said, still grinning.

"Who?"

"Maria Sanchez, who'll be taking over my job, will be in Pinecrest for the weekend."

"Jillian's friend?"

"Yeah. She's coming into town to check things out before she moves up here at the end of October right before I leave."

His last statement reminded Beth that this guy was temporary. Here today and gone tomorrow. That should serve to keep her from wanting things that just couldn't be. Like a relationship with this man. Too many things stood as barriers between them. "I still can't go. I can't leave Max. Besides, he's got a football game on Friday."

"Got that figured out. We go to the game on Friday night in Colville. Then we head over to the resort. Sam's parents are keeping Brian and Kim's boys for that weekend. They said Max could stay with them as well."

"Max is really going to think being lumped in with a couple of six-year-olds is great. Every teenage boy's dream weekend."

Clay didn't miss the sarcasm that returned to Beth's voice. "The Lawsons said Max could help them babysit. Let me talk to him."

"Why are you so insistent that I go?"

"Because we enjoy your company. And it will give you a chance to get to know Maria. She'll be moving in upstairs after I leave. And, more importantly, I'm still hoping you'll connect with the church again."

Beth had to give him points for one thing. He was honest. No beating around the bush. "When I think church, I picture a lot of hypocrites. People saying one thing and doing another."

"Are you thinking of Jillian's nephew Dylan?"

Beth shrugged. "Not necessarily. It's more than that. I've had some bad experiences myself, and I don't want to repeat them."

"So you stay away just waiting to see whether we mess up."

"You're putting words in my mouth."

"I don't mean to do that. None of us is perfect, Beth. You're sure to find us doing something we shouldn't. Give us a chance. Give God a chance. People might fail, but God doesn't."

"Sometimes I wish I could believe that." She gazed at her plate and worried that she'd revealed too much.

"So you'll go?"

Maybe if she said yes he would be satisfied with that. "I'll give it some thought, but there's still that matter of Max."

"I'll take care of that right now." Clay hopped up and crossed the yard to where Max sat with Brittany.

What would Max say when presented with the idea of spending the weekend with Kim's little boys? She somehow doubted that he would agree to it. But lately Max seemed swayed by whatever Clay said.

Watching the animated conversation between Max and Clay, she thought of how much she loved her son. She wanted to provide Max with everything he wanted or needed. That was her goal in life. She wanted the best for him, but one thing he wanted she couldn't provide. A father. A complete family. One with grandparents as well as parents. Scott had refused to acknowledge her to his parents. Could she ever reconcile with her own? She wasn't even sure where they lived. She was beginning to realize that depriving Max of his grandparents was something she might live to regret. But fear of their rejecting him had kept her from trying to reconnect with them over the years.

She had tried her best to tell Max good things about his father. And she'd told him truthfully that Scott was killed in a motorcycle accident before he was born. But how could she explain to a young boy about a teen father who hadn't wanted to acknowledge his own son? And she had only told Max that she didn't get along with her parents. Thankfully, Max had quit asking questions about his dad, and he'd never seemed to miss having grandparents.

While those thoughts raced around in her brain, Clay returned. An image of him and Max as father and son came unbidden to her mind. The thought was foolish and unrealistic, because Clay would soon be gone. There was nothing permanent about his presence in Max's life.

"Good news," Clay said as he resumed his seat. "Max thought it was a great idea. And on that Saturday he wants to go with Brittany's family to watch her at some mini-cheerleading competition that's a warm-up for one of the big official competitions later in the year. Has he mentioned that to you?"

Beth took in the new information. Great. Now Max was making plans without her knowledge and telling Clay. But she didn't want Clay to know that. So she wouldn't give him a direct answer. "So now I suppose you expect me to say yes to this retreat thing."

"I would like you to go, but the decision is yours."

He was putting it fully in her lap. "How much does it cost? Sounds expensive."

"Your only expense will be the cost of your train ticket." Clay leaned forward in his chair. "You don't have to tell me now. Just let me know for sure by next weekend."

"Sure." Beth pasted a smile on her face. Now he would go tell Kim of her supposed interest. Then Kim would try to persuade her to go. She sighed. Sometimes it was just easier to go along than put up resistance. She had to admit that despite her initial opposition she had enjoyed the camping trip. But that was because of Max. And he wouldn't be there this time.

Later that evening, Kim, sporting a big grin, approached Beth. "Hey, I heard you're going to go on the retreat with us. That's great. I'm so glad."

With a sigh, Beth resigned herself to attending the retreat. Somehow she was going to have to deal with Clay and the way he made her feel. And with God. The stuff with Clay was temporary and wouldn't matter once he was gone. But God was a different matter. How long could she continue to ignore Him?

The following Wednesday evening Beth swept leaves off the front porch while streetlights glowed in the twilight that surrounded the house. The air had grown cooler with the setting of the sun. Beth shivered and retreated to the house. She put on a jacket and stepped out the door. As she picked up her broom, a gray sedan pulled to the curb.

Max jumped out of the car and bounded up the steps. "Hey, Mom."

Beth stopped sweeping and leaned on the broom. "Hey, yourself. Are you done with your teen meeting already?"

"Not exactly." He stopped and looked at her.

Beth tightened her grip on the broom handle. "What do you mean?"

"Mom, please be happy for me."

"Why wouldn't I be happy for you?"

"Because I accepted Jesus as my savior tonight." Max motioned to the car as the words tumbled from his mouth. "Mr. and Mrs. Banks are taking me back to the church. I'm going to be baptized, and I want you to be there."

Beth's mind whirled with the implications as she stared at her son. She had said attending church was his decision. Had she thought this wouldn't happen? Would he live to regret this decision as she had? So much heartache went with her youthful church experiences. She didn't want Max to suffer that same hurt. What could she say? She couldn't refuse his request. Her presence apparently meant a lot to him.

"Okay, honey. If that's what you want."

"Thanks, Mom." He gave her a big, exuberant hug. "You can just come with us now. Okay?"

"Sure. After I lock up, I'll be right out."

"Great." Max raced down the steps.

Minutes later Beth followed Max into the church auditorium. A group of teens sat near the front. While she stood there surveying the room, several adults, whom she had seen from time to time, filed into the pew behind the teens.

She turned to Max. "Where do you want me to sit?"

"You can sit with us." Beth turned at the sound of Kim's voice behind her. Kim embraced her and whispered in her ear. "I know you might have your reservations about this, but we are so happy for Max."

Stepping out of Kim's embrace, Beth tried to smile. "Show me where to sit."

"Let's go right up front." Kim motioned to Brian, who had just walked in the side door with their twin boys.

The boys raced toward Beth and nearly tackled her in a hug. She smiled as Brian grinned and shook his head. "Sorry about that. They're excited to see you."

Beth joined Kim and her family in the front pew. "I can't believe how many people are here."

"When Ted and Marci called Pastor Craig to tell him that Max wanted to be baptized, they started the phone calls using the prayer chain to let people know. Lots of people care about Max and wanted to be here for his baptism."

Beth's heart swelled with pride at Kim's statement, but she worried for Max. Could he live up to their lofty expectations? She hadn't.

Quiet conversation filtered through the auditorium as more people arrived. Memories crowded Beth's mind. The last time she had sat in a front pew at church, she had been ten years old and nervous about reciting the verses she had worked so diligently to memorize. When her turn came, she had stood before the congregation and reeled off the verses in record time.

But she had received no accolades from her father, just a comment that she had spoken too fast. No matter how hard she had tried, nothing pleased him. Finally she had decided to please herself, but in the end that had only led to trouble and more disappointment. She didn't want that for Max, but how could she spare him?

While Beth stewed, one of the men in the congregation stood up to lead some songs. Beth listened to the voices raised in harmony as they sang the unfamiliar chorus. Despite her resistance, the song about an awesome God touched her heart. Not wanting that, she pushed the feeling away. She wouldn't let herself be drawn in again—only to be hurt again. She steeled her heart against any emotion as more anthems filled the air.

Just as one of the songs ended, Max and Pastor Craig appeared in the baptistry at the front of the auditorium. Beth watched with pride and trepidation as Pastor Craig said the words from her youth and lowered Max into the water. The smile on Max's face when he came up brought tears to her eyes. She blinked them back. She wanted to feel nothing. Nothing, so she wouldn't be sucked into believing she could find happiness in a church again.

The congregation applauded, and the song leader led another chorus. This time a familiar song about sins being blotted out rang through the auditorium. The message from the song pricked Beth's soul. She clutched the top of the pew in front of her until her knuckles were white. Could *her* sins be blotted out? Even after she had turned her back on God all these years?

Sam came forward and said a prayer for Max. Beth fought the urge to pray, too. *Don't let these church people hurt Max.* She pushed the thought away. God probably didn't listen to prayers from people like her.

After Pastor Craig said a final prayer, the congregation stood. Joyous laughter and talking echoed around Beth. She tried to smile as Kim gave her another hug.

"Now that Max has turned his life over to God, what about you?" Kim peered at Beth. "I've been praying for you."

Beth shook her head. "I've strayed too far to come back now."

"God's a big God. He's patient and wants everyone to be saved. He's waiting for you, Beth."

Beth looked up. "Please don't preach at me, Kim."

"I wasn't meaning to preach."

"It seemed like that to me."

"Okay, I won't mention it again, but I won't stop praying."

"As far as I'm concerned, you're wasting your breath."

Before Beth could say anything else, Max appeared, his hair still slightly damp. He put an arm around her shoulders and gave them a squeeze. "Thanks for coming, Mom. I'm glad you were here."

She smiled, her first genuine smile of the night. "I'm glad I was here, too."

Soon well-wishers surrounded Max, and Beth was glad to escape off to one side. But not for long. Her heart skipped a beat as Clay approached, a serious look on his face. She prepared herself for more preaching.

"Hi. How are you doing?"

"Okay." What was he really asking? Did he want to know how she felt in general or how she felt about what Max had just done? She couldn't read between the lines or tell by his expression.

"Great. I just wanted to let you know Ted and Marci Banks, who lead the mid-week teen study, want to take the kids over to the Pinecrest Café to celebrate Max's decision. Jillian, Sam and I are also going. Would you like to come?"

No. She didn't want to put herself right in the middle of this gathering to celebrate something she wasn't sure about. Besides, what kid would want his mother crashing his party?

Thankfully, before she had to answer, Max appeared. "Hey, Mom, is it okay if I go with everyone to the Pinecrest Café?"

"Yeah. That's fine, as long as you get all your homework done."

"I did that before I left tonight."

"Okay, but be home by eleven."

"I'll probably be home by ten." He waved. "See you later."

Beth turned back to Clay. "I think I'd be intruding if I went with you. He doesn't need his mother along. None of the other kids will have parents there."

"I see your point. You're a very perceptive mom. Max is lucky to have you." He gave her a smile.

"Thanks." Why was he being so agreeable? His silence regarding her response to the evening's events bothered her more than Kim's prodding. Maybe Kim was right. All those prayers were starting to work.

"Do you need a ride home?"

She shook her head. "I'll catch a ride with Kim and Brian."

"Okay, but don't forget the adults will have their turn to party soon." He winked. "Right?"

She nodded as she took in the reminder of the upcoming retreat. She had agreed to go and now wondered why. But deep down inside she knew she was going because of Clay.

When they first met, he had made her nervous, but now he made her smile even when she didn't want to. He seemed to sense when she was down and would coax her into a better mood with his corny jokes. She was even used to him popping in with a pizza for her and Max or just dropping by to see how her day had gone. He helped Max with his schoolwork and her with chores around her apartment. She couldn't deny it any longer. He had subtly insinuated himself into her thoughts and her life. How would she deal with it when he was gone?

Chapter Ten

"All aboard!"

The conductor's call signaled the beginning of the retreat's sightseeing train ride. While a whistle blew, the train creaked and pulled away from the station. Beth sat next to a window and tried not to look at Clay, who sat with Maria Sanchez across the aisle and up one row of seats.

Beth's chest felt as though a large hand were squeezing the life out of it. She didn't want to admit she might be jealous that Clay was laughing and talking with Maria, a beautiful brunette with dark, expressive eyes and a wide smile. Beth had spent practically every day since she met Clay wishing he would go away. Now that his attention was on someone else, she realized she didn't really want that. She hadn't wanted his interest until someone else claimed it. How juvenile. How stupid. How middle school.

Besides, Clay and Maria were just getting reacquainted, weren't they? They had business to discuss. Why should she care? But Beth couldn't deny that she did. Despite all the times she had told herself not to be interested in Clay, she was. Her silly heart raced every time she looked at him.

A litany of Clay's good qualities romped through her mind. His kindness had surfaced every time he helped her over the past couple of months. He always showed genuine concern about Max. Even Clay's most annoying habit of urging her to reconsider her relationship with God and the church showed his interest.

But did he care in a way that meant more than friendship? In the beginning she had thought he was just like Max's father. Over time she had learned otherwise. But she had been afraid of her feelings. She didn't trust herself when his mischievous grin made her pulse gallop and her stomach do little flip-flops.

But what difference did it make anyway? He would be gone in no time. He had come to town with *temporary* stamped on his forehead. She should keep that in mind when she worried about whether he might get involved with Maria.

"What a spectacular view of the river." Kim tapped Beth on the shoulder.

Glad for the conversation to take her thoughts away from Clay, Beth nodded.

"I love this adults-only weekend," Kim continued. "I can enjoy myself without worrying about keeping the boys under control. They can be a handful at times."

"Wait until they get to be teenagers. Then you'll really have something to worry about." Beth sighed. "Max wants to get his learner's permit to drive! I'm not ready for that."

"That is a big step."

"I told him he could get it when he saved enough money to pay for half of his driver's training classes."

Kim chuckled. "So that's why he keeps asking everyone at church whether they needed any yard work done."

"I had no idea he was doing that. I'll tell him not to bug people."

"It's okay. It shows he has initiative."

"I know, but he shouldn't make a pest of himself."

"Beth, your son is not a pest in any sense of the word. I just wish…" Pausing, Kim gave Beth an impish grin. "Oh, I promised I wouldn't say anything more about that. So I'll just be quiet."

Kim didn't have to finish her thought for Beth to know what she meant. She wasn't going to mention Beth's relationship to God or church. But Kim didn't have to because this whole weekend was dedicated to these people's relationship to God. And without a doubt, they wanted her to be a part of that.

Resistance was getting harder and harder to come by. Sometimes she wondered why she fought so hard against God. Other times she knew without a doubt. She couldn't get over the hurts she'd suffered at the hands of people who said they loved God. Fear froze her.

Beth remained silent as she took in the golden aspens along the banks of the Pend Oreille River. The train wound its way along the cliffs high above the water. Breathtaking scenery filled every vista. The train suddenly seemed to be suspended in air as it crossed a bridge that spanned the river, and the ground temporarily disappeared. They slowed to a stop. Clicking shutters filled the air as people snapped pictures of the river valley and the view of the distant hills arrayed in gold and yellow. She pulled a disposable camera from her pocket and joined the frenzy.

"Did you get enough pictures?"

Beth's heart jumped at the sound of Clay's voice. She nodded, unable to speak for a moment. She let the camera dangle from the cord around her wrist. "I did."

"Me, too." He held up an expensive-looking digital camera. "I bought this just for this trip. You want to see?"

"Sure."

The whistle sounded, almost drowning out her answer. The train resumed its journey to Metaline Falls. Clay motioned for Beth to sit beside him on the upholstered seat. They sat shoulder to shoulder, their heads bowed over the camera while they viewed image after image on the little screen. Beth forced herself to think about the photos instead of the way her heart was thumping in rhythm with the clickety-clack of the train.

They finished viewing the pictures as the train plunged into a tunnel in the mountain. When they emerged on the other side, Clay stood. "Keep looking out the window. We might see some deer."

"Okay." Before gazing out the window, Beth glanced around and saw Maria talking with Jillian and Sam. Why had Clay abandoned his seat next to Maria?

Forget about Clay. Just enjoy the picturesque scenery. While the train weaved its way through the forest, the breathtaking views of the rusts, golds and yellows sprinkled through the evergreens awed her. As Clay predicted, two white-tailed deer hovered near the tracks before bounding back into the woods.

"Wow! Did you see them?" She turned to Clay.

"Yes," he said, snapping her picture.

"Why'd you do that?"

"I wanted to capture the look on your face. Your expression was priceless. You looked like a kid on Christmas morning."

"Don't make fun of me."

"I wasn't making fun. I loved seeing the wonder in your eyes." He put an arm around her shoulders and drew her close.

Warmth crept up her cheeks. All coherent thought fled. Why was he acting this way? Was he deliberately saying things to catch her off guard? Make her feel that he cared? She struck the thoughts from her mind. Why was she always comparing Clay to Max's dad? She had to get it through her head that they were nothing alike. Clay would never use her the way Scott Harkin had.

Finally gaining her equilibrium, she gave him a tentative smile. "Let me see it."

He promptly displayed the picture on the screen. "See what I mean? Look at you. Awe all over your face. And besides that, it's a great picture."

Beth examined her image. He was right. She had never considered herself photogenic, but the sunlight in her hair made it look almost blond. And the backdrop of fall foliage highlighted her eyes. "Could I get a copy of that?"

"Sure. When I get prints made, I'll give you one."

"Thanks." She tried not to read anything into the fact that he would have a picture of her as a memento of this trip.

The train chugged along until it came to a stop in Metaline Falls. While the engine was moved to the other end of the train for the return journey, a group of local actors, posing as the Cutter gang, boarded the train and proceeded to "rob" the passengers in the form of soliciting donations for the Cutter Theatre.

Clay remained seated beside her as the train started back to Ione. "I'm looking forward to their mystery dinner theater tonight. How about you?"

"Sounds like fun. I've never been to one of those."

"Now aren't you glad I insisted you come?"

Beth hated to admit he was right. "Is this your way of saying I told you so?"

"No." He gave her a lopsided grin. "I just wanted to be sure you were having a good time."

"I am."

For the remainder of the trip Beth turned her attention once again to the scenery and tried to ignore Clay's presence. But from time to time he leaned closer as he pointed out something along the way. Her heart raced every time their shoulders touched.

By the time the group had arrived back at the resort near the river, Beth's insides were tied into knots of tension. She had let her mind roam around and around her feelings for Clay and her relationship to God and the church until she felt almost nauseated. She wanted to be by herself and gather her thoughts.

The church van that had brought them from the train pulled to a stop in the parking lot of the resort. Beth scrambled out and hoped no one would follow her. She scurried away until she reached the river's edge. She turned to see whether anyone had noticed her departure. She breathed a sigh of relief. No one was looking in her direction.

She didn't know what to make of Clay's attention.

From the very beginning he had befriended her. She wasn't used to receiving much interest from men. She had dated some when Max was younger, but as soon as her dates found out she had a kid, they didn't ask her out again. Clearly she didn't know how to pick the right kind of guys. So she figured she was better off without them.

Her thoughts about men often spilled over into her thoughts about people in general. She was wary of forming attachments with anyone, even these kind people who always wanted to include her in their plans. She knew they wanted her to be part of the church, but was that so bad? It must mean they thought she had something to contribute. She had to quit questioning people's motives. These folks were her friends. Friends. That's what she had wanted her whole life. A place to belong and friends to go with it. She had realized that dream in Pinecrest, but would it last if she continued to live on the fringes of church life?

Clay closed the van and pocketed the keys. Driving everyone back from Ione had made it impossible to talk privately with Beth. Now he didn't see her. Everything about this weekend muddled his mind. Time was racing away from him. Soon he'd be gone, and there was so much unfinished business he was leaving behind. All of it involving Beth Carlson. He was torn in so many directions.

Thoughts of Beth constantly bombarded his mind. He couldn't shake the picture of her preserved on his camera. Despite his best efforts not to let it happen, as easily as he had captured her picture, she had captured his heart. There was no denying it. Now he had to leave. And he hadn't been able to bring her back to the Lord.

Until she found her way back to God, Clay couldn't pursue her. He had to make another effort to persuade her to give her life back to the Lord. But would she listen?

If she did, how would he feel about living in a small town like Pinecrest? Ever since he'd left his own hometown, he had vowed never to live in a small town again. Now here he was, thinking of doing just that because of a woman. A woman he wasn't sure even liked him that much. Could he ever sort all this out?

As he started toward the lodge, he spied Beth standing at the edge of the river, which reflected the sky and the hillsides of evergreens silhouetted against the colorful sunset. The feeling in his heart at the sight of her matched the glorious reds and golds spread across the sky.

Taking in the beauty of God's creation, Clay headed toward Beth. "Hey, I wondered where you had gone." She turned, and his pulse pounded. "I wanted to ask you something."

"What?" For a moment she didn't look glad to see him, but then she smiled that sweet, shy little smile that turned him inside out.

How he was going to miss that smile. He was going to miss everything about her. "Tomorrow, when we leave…" He rubbed the back of his neck. How was he going to convince her to go with him when she hated motorcycles? Finally, he blurted, "Will you ride back to Pinecrest with me?"

She stared at him as if she had heard him incorrectly. "Ride back with you?"

"Yeah, I want to—Sam told me about this great little picnic area just north of here. And it's supposed to be warm tomorrow. And I just wondered…" Oh, man. He looked away toward the river. He was babbling. This was so bad. He hadn't been this tongue-tied around a female since he'd been in middle school, when he had a crush on his English teacher. He shook his head. "I know you don't like motorcycles, but—"

"Clay, are you asking me to go on a picnic with you?"

He glanced back at her, and she was smiling. A big smile. He laughed, feeling the tension flow out of his shoulders. "Yes. Will you go?"

"Yes."

Beth waved good-bye to Kim and Brian as the couple drove away from the resort. Then, turning to Clay, who stood next to his motorcycle, she plastered a smile on her face and hoped he couldn't tell how nervous she was. When she had accepted his invitation yesterday to take this ride, she had decided to put old fears behind her. Fears about motorcycles. Fears about her feelings for Clay. Fears about God. Taking this ride was part of that effort.

Smiling at her, Clay straddled the bike and settled on the leather seat. The full impact of this expedition hit her like the sun glinting off the handlebars. She was going to spend the rest of the day with her arms wrapped around the torso of a man she had tried to dislike since she'd first met him. Now she had to face the reality. Despite her resistance, he had won her heart. But hadn't she decided not to run away from her feelings anymore?

"Ready?" Clay held out a helmet to her.

"Yeah." She took the helmet and put it on. Climbing aboard, she took a deep breath before she put her arms around him.

Clay shifted his weight, and his muscles rippled within her embrace. When he started the motorcycle, the noise of the engine covered the pounding of her heart.

"Hang on!" he yelled over the sound. "Relax."

"Easy for you to say. I'm not used to this. How far are we going?"

"I don't know the exact mileage, but once we get on highway twenty, we go north. We'll stop in Ione and pick up something for the picnic."

After he drove onto the main road, they picked up speed. Despite the sunshine warming the fall day, she was glad for her jacket that warded off the chill produced by the speed of the bike. She tried to concentrate on the trees lining the road, but she had little luck calming the swirling sensation in her midsection. She wanted to attribute the feeling to the ride, but without a doubt Clay was the cause.

When they reached Ione, they stopped at a store for picnic supplies. After packing their purchases in the compartments on the bike, they drove through the tiny town, graced by beautiful stands of golden aspen and maples.

As they headed north, the highway followed the river much as the railroad did but provided a different perspective. The Pend Oreille River reflected the cottonwood trees and golden aspens.

Once they reached the picnic area, Clay pulled off the highway. Getting off the bike, he removed his helmet and hung it on one of the handlebars. Then he held out a hand to her and grinned. "Well, how did it go? Did you enjoy the ride?"

Smiling, she took his hand as he helped her off the bike. "The scenery's great. But I'm still not real comfortable riding that bike."

"You don't have to tell me. You were crushing my ribs."

"Sorry." She removed her helmet and chuckled, enjoying his company more than she ever thought she would.

He reached over and tucked several strands of hair, which had escaped from her red scrunchy, behind one ear. Their gazes met and held. Her heart skittered, and she nearly forgot to breathe. Was he going to kiss her? She wasn't ready for that.

Before he could do anything, she broke eye contact and turned back to the motorcycle. She removed her jacket and draped it over the seat. "I'm hungry. Let's eat."

"Me, too." Clay helped her get the sandwiches, apples and drinks. He handed her one of each. Motioning for her to join him, he headed to one of the picnic tables dotting the wooded area. Sunlight filtered through the evergreens, giving the area a dappled, fairyland appearance.

He slid onto one of the benches and patted the space beside him. "Have a seat."

"Sure." She sat next to him, unwrapped her sandwich and took a bite.

Eating was safe. Looking at Clay was not. All the old insecurities crept back into her mind. She chewed slowly and hoped he didn't expect any sparkling conversation. What was she doing here when he was leaving Pinecrest so soon? Maybe that's *why* she had come. She knew their time together was limited, so there couldn't be a relationship that would eventually break her heart.

Or had she already stepped over that line and just didn't want to admit it?

Chapter Eleven

Clay watched Beth out of the corner of his eye while he ate. Was she having a good time? She had been quiet all day. Riding a motorcycle didn't lend itself to conversation, but even when they had stopped at the store and looked around, she hadn't said but a few words. He wanted her to enjoy the day, not just the beautiful surroundings but being with him.

He had let the weeks go by without making a move. And there had been good reason for that. She didn't share his faith. But with Max accepting Jesus as his savior, Clay was sure Beth had been rethinking her own relationship to God. He wanted her to come back to the Lord. He had to admit part of that feeling came from his attraction to her. He couldn't shake it. It clung in his mind like the moss on the north side of the trees.

Until she had agreed to come with him today, she had tried to shut him out. Why? Did her reluctance have something to do with Max's dad? Had they been teenage lovers, and his death had torn them apart? Had she loved him so deeply that she couldn't think of loving someone else? Or had she been hurt so badly that she was afraid to love again? Clay wanted to know.

He wished she would talk about her past. Share the hurts and pain with him. He wanted to learn about her so he could understand what had brought her to this point. He hoped that somehow he could be part of her life.

They ate in silence as he searched for just the right question to start the conversation. He felt as inadequate as a teenage boy on his first date. Finally he asked, "So, are you glad there's only one more football game left in the season?"

Nodding, she smiled that familiar little smile. "You bet. And I'm glad Max hasn't played that much."

"What are you going to do next year when he's a starter?"

"You think that will happen?"

Clay grinned. "Sure. He's got the potential to be a great receiver, and the coaches know it."

"I wish he didn't like football," she said with a sigh.

"Then why did you let him play?"

"Because I want him to have the opportunities I didn't have."

"You mean you wanted to play football?" He chuckled.

"No." She gave him an irritated glance. "Softball. Remember?"

"Yeah. Your parents wouldn't let you play."

"They didn't let me do a lot of things. Eventually I got tired of it and did what I wanted." Without warning, she picked up their sandwich wrappers and headed for the nearby trash barrel.

"Does this mean an end to our conversation?" Clay called after her.

She stopped and turned. "Yes."

Clay jumped up and followed her. "Are you running away from me again?"

"Why would you say that?" She gave him a sidelong glance.

"Because yesterday you jumped out of the van like it was on fire. But I still found you. And you agreed to come with me today. Why?"

She looked at him for what seemed like forever without giving him an answer. "Because I wanted to be with you." Lowering her head, she broke eye contact. "But part of me is scared of getting too close. All my life, when I let someone get too close…well, I've learned to keep my distance."

Her anguish tore him apart. Wanting to take away her pain, he pulled her into his arms. She felt fragile in his embrace. Slipping her arms around his waist, she laid her head against his chest. When her shoulders started to shake, he realized she was crying. He held her and stroked her back.

As her tears wet his shirt, he wrapped her more tightly in his arms and remained silent. He wasn't sure what he could say. Did her tears have something to do with Max's father? She had made sketchy comments about her teen years, but she danced around any further discussion of them like water on a hot griddle. Could he get her to reveal more? He decided on the direct approach. "Would you like to talk?"

Stepping out of his embrace, she wiped the tears from her eyes and cheeks. She sniffled. "I…I don't know."

He reached into his pocket and pulled out a paper napkin. "Left over from lunch."

"Thanks." She used the napkin and then stuffed it into her pocket. "Sorry I blubbered all over you." She touched the wet spot her tears had left on his shirt.

The simple touch of her fingers was like a hot brand. He covered her hand with his, pressing her fingers to his chest. Their gazes locked. He was sure she could feel the pounding of his heart beneath her hand. He wanted to kiss her, but he didn't want to scare her away.

"Talk to me, Beth. Tell me what makes you cry."

"Why? Why should I reveal my deep, dark secrets to you?" she asked with a feeble attempt at humor.

"Sometimes you just need to talk things over with someone. And I'd like to be that someone." Holding her at arm's length, he placed his hands on her shoulders.

She shook her head. "Not now. Let's just go look at the falls."

"Okay," he agreed, reluctant to pressure her. He fell into step beside her as they walked the trail. Would she ever open up to him? He didn't know, but he sensed that not pushing her was the best thing he could do right now.

While they walked through the forest, Clay took her hand. A warm sensation filled his chest when she looked at him and smiled. *Lord, You know how I feel about Beth. Help me to do and say the right things that will turn her heart to You.*

The trail wound its way along a creek among the tall pines and narrowed to a gravel footpath as the woods grew closer. When they reached the top of the trail, Clay put an arm around Beth's shoulders. They stood on the creek bank and watched the water cascade down the rocky hillside. Sunlight trickled through the trees and danced on the falls. Contentment settled around Clay's heart. He wished he weren't leaving this scenic area, and marveled that he would even think about staying.

Looking around, Beth took a deep breath and let out what seemed to be a blissful sigh. "It's beautiful here. So peaceful."

"I'm glad Sam told me about this place." Clay pulled his camera out of his pocket. "Let me take your picture."

"Haven't you taken enough pictures of me already?"

"No. Never enough."

"I hate having my picture taken."

"Just look at the waterfall and forget I'm here."

"How can I forget you're here?" She frowned at him.

"You're having a hard time forgetting me? I like that."

Beth laughed and waved a hand at him. "The pictures are going to be awful."

"Oh, no. They're going to be wonderful."

"I'm leaving." She started down the trail.

He bounded around her and took a picture of her descending the hill. As the trail widened, Beth raced around him and ran toward the motorcycle. Clay chased after her and caught her just as she reached the bike. He pulled her into his arms.

Kissing her was all he could think about, but he resisted. His heart raced while he held her. How was he ever going to leave her behind? If only he could get her to open up to him. If only he could get her to see how much the Lord loved her.

He swallowed hard and took a deep breath. He let it out slowly. "Beth, I care about you. I care a lot."

She stepped out of his embrace and looked up at him. "But you don't really know me. So how can you care?"

"What I do know makes me care. You're a great mother to Max. You're wonderful with kids. You'll make a fabulous teacher. And I can tell you're a caring friend."

"You'd probably change your mind if you knew my whole story."

"Nothing you can tell me will change the way I feel about you."

"It will."

"Try me."

"I don't want you to think I'm awful." She turned away and didn't say anything for several moments. Then slowly she turned back to him. "Besides, I don't want to cry again."

"I won't think you're awful. And crying we can handle." He rummaged through a compartment on the bike and came up bearing a handful of tissues. "You're all set. Talk away."

Smiling weakly, she took the tissues. "Where do I begin?"

Glad to see her smile, and thrilled that she was willing to talk about herself, he led the way back to where they had eaten their lunch. He patted the bench beside him. "Sit down, and start at the beginning."

She stared at him, her blue eyes shining with tears. "The beginning of what? My life?"

"The beginning of whatever it is that makes you so sad."

Sighing heavily, she looked past him into the distance. "There's not one specific thing. It's a lot of things all jumbled together. It's the way I messed up my life. I grew up with rules. Unfortunately, I broke most of them. So I was no longer accepted. I'm still not."

"Even in Pinecrest?"

Beth shrugged. "I'm afraid to find out what people really think of me."

"People in general or church people?"

"Church people."

"Tell me what makes you feel this way."

She twisted her hands in her lap. She still didn't look him in the eye. "When I was younger I tried to please my parents, especially my dad, but nothing I ever did was good enough."

"How did he make you feel that way?"

Shifting her position, she again looked off into the distance. "He made me feel all my choices were dumb. I decided I could never live up to his expectations, so why try? I defied him by sneaking off to be with Max's dad."

Clay had had similar thoughts about his own father. Would it help if he told her that? Maybe. But before he told his story, he had to learn more about her. "What does your father think now?"

"I wouldn't know." She shrugged. "I haven't talked to my parents in years."

"You haven't?"

"No. They didn't want anything to do with me after Max was born. They've never even met him."

Clay hoped the shock didn't show on his face. Despite the problems he'd had with his own parents, especially his father, Clay couldn't imagine never seeing them. "Didn't they ever talk to you after that?"

Lowering her gaze, Beth shook her head. "We communicated a little in the beginning through my great-aunt, but my parents were even angry at her. Eventually we lost touch."

"Why were they mad at your aunt?"

"Because when they sent me to live with her, I was supposed to give Max up for adoption after he was born. But I didn't want to give him up." Beth bit her lower lip and closed her eyes as if she was trying to fight back tears. Letting out a long, slow breath, she finally opened her eyes. "My great-aunt understood. She made it possible for me to keep Max. That angered my parents and basically ended all communication between us."

"Why did your great-aunt go against your parents?"

"She loved me, and she knew how much I wanted to keep Max. In fact, Max is named after her."

"Her name was Max?"

Beth laughed. "No. Her name was Violet Maxwell."

"So Max's full name is Maxwell?"

"Yeah, but I only call him that when I'm angry." She laughed a little.

Clay drank in the sound of her laughter. It was so much better than her tears. He hated to see her sad, but he wanted to know more. "What about Max's dad? Max told me he was killed in a motorcycle accident. Is that why you're wary of bikes?"

Her eyes narrowed. Even behind the glasses he didn't miss the flash of pain in her beautiful blue eyes. "Max's dad." She paused and sighed heavily. "He told me he loved me, and I was stupid enough to believe him."

"What have you told Max?"

"Just that his father is dead. I hate to say it, but Scott Harkin wasn't a very nice person. I realize now he was a spoiled rich kid who'd learned he could use people. And I was so dumb. I fell for his charm without ever seeing the real person behind the popular, handsome athlete. But I wouldn't tell Max that. So I've said very little."

Clay's heart twisted. What would she say if she knew she was describing the person he had once been? "Does Max ever ask about his dad?"

"He did when he was younger, but not lately."

"So you lived with your great-aunt until you moved to Pinecrest?"

"Yeah. When I first went to live with her, she was in wonderful health. She was retired but always on the go, doing volunteer or charity work. Eventually she became Max's caregiver while I worked and went to school."

"You went back to high school?"

Beth shook her head. "No. I got my GED and then took classes at the local community college whenever I could. I worked at a neighborhood school as a teacher's aide. The same kind of job I have now."

"You said your aunt died?"

Tears welling in her eyes again, Beth nodded. "Yeah. "When Max was eleven, she had a stroke. So unexpected. It left her bedridden. I took care of her until she died a year and a half later."

"Didn't your parents come to her funeral?"

"No. They were in the middle of a two-year mission trip to Costa Rica. My maternal grandmother, my great-aunt's sister, told me at the funeral."

"So you talked with your grandmother?"

"Yes."

"Did she give you any message from your parents?"

"No. My parents pretty much didn't want anything to do with me." She looked away. "I was an embarrassment to them."

Clay's heart ached as he listened to Beth's story. Surely if they saw the respectable life she had made for herself, they would change their minds. And they had a healthy, handsome grandson. How could they throw that away? Clay wanted to make everything right in Beth's life. Take away her sadness. "Have you tried to contact them?"

"I don't have any idea where they are. When I left home, they were living in a small town in Ohio. I've managed without them for this long. I don't see any need to contact them now."

"Doesn't Max ever ask about them?"

"Oh, every once in a while. But not in a long time. It's just as well. I don't want them to hurt him, too."

Clay understood more and more Beth's reluctance to be part of the church. Supposedly Christian people had hurt her badly. What kind of parents turned away from their only child forever? Deep in his heart Clay knew from experience that Beth needed reconciliation with God *and* her parents. Was there any way to bring that about? Prayer and lots of it might be the only answer. "How would you feel if they tried to contact you now?"

Beth's eyes widened as she pushed up her glasses. "I don't know. If they came looking for me this very minute and found us sitting here talking, they would probably turn around and walk away."

"Why?"

She studied him with that little smile curving her mouth, a mouth he found harder and harder to resist kissing. "Because my dad would take one look at you and figure I was still hanging around with the bad boys. He definitely wouldn't be fond of that hair."

"Even though I plan to give it to a worthy cause?"

"Yeah. He's a by-the-book kind of guy. There is a set

of rules that you just don't fool with in his opinion. Long hair on guys is just one of those rules. Step outside the lines, and you're on his black list."

Clay figured this was the time to tell his own story. "We have a lot more in common than you think, you know."

She shook her head. "Not possible."

"Yes, we do. My dad was also, as you say, 'a by-the-book kind of guy.' We were at odds for years. Almost until he died. He dropped dead of a heart attack just weeks after I finally swallowed my pride and went to talk to him. Best thing I ever did."

Skepticism shone in Beth's expression. "Are you saying I should try to reconcile with my parents?"

"First you need to reconcile with God, then your parents. That's what happened with me."

"And you think your experience is like mine?" She shook her head. "I doubt it. *You* made the decision not to associate with your parents, right? You weren't sent away."

"That's true, but—"

"There are no buts," she interrupted. "I thought my parents would help me. But they turned away from me. My father was worried that if word got out about my pregnancy, his ministry would be affected. He couldn't have that. He yelled and berated me, telling me I didn't know how to use the good sense God had given me. Then he shipped me off to stay with my great-aunt because she lived half a country away here in Washington."

Clay sighed. "You're right. My parents didn't kick me out of the house, but they made it miserable to be there. They showed up at church each Sunday, but at home they fought constantly. My dad lorded it over everyone, so I did just the opposite of what he wanted. Rebellion was my middle name."

"I remember your testimony at the Labor Day campout. You said Jillian helped change your life. How?"

"Yeah. I'd never met someone like her. She showed me what true Christianity was all about. It isn't a bunch of rules. Or even going to church every Sunday. It's about loving and caring for people the way Jesus did."

"The rules. My dad was good about preaching the rules."

Clay wished he knew how to convince her to trust in God again. "Beth, maybe our experiences aren't exactly the same, but we have a lot in common. If God can forgive me and give me a new life, He can do it for you, too."

"I don't know…." She looked away. "I doubt I can be good enough."

"It's not about being good enough. It's about God's grace."

"I don't know about grace. Grace was always some kind of murky concept to me."

"His grace blots out our sins. He doesn't remember them anymore."

"But people do."

"Yeah. That's true. But we can't rely only on people. We have to rely on God. Look at some of the characters in the Bible. Samson fought lust. Noah got drunk. David stole somebody's wife. But the book of Hebrews says that they all died in faith. Christians can struggle, too, but God is always willing to take us back. He wants to forgive us."

"I wish I could believe that, but I'm afraid to try." She jumped up from the bench and ran to his motorcycle.

Clay hurried after her. "What's wrong?"

"Let's just go." She grabbed her helmet and shoved it on her head. "I don't want to talk anymore."

Putting on his own helmet, he didn't argue. There was no point in it. She had made up her mind to resist. Maybe for now the fact that she wouldn't listen anymore was a good sign. Something he said had touched her, and she was running scared. He could only pray that the message of God's forgiveness and grace would penetrate her resistance and fears.

As the motorcycle sped down the highway, Beth tried to block Clay's words from her mind. They were too persuasive. She wanted to accept and believe them, but doing that would require stripping away the barriers she had built around her heart. She had taken enough chances already today.

This trip signified her willingness to step out of her comfort zone. First, agreeing to come with Clay. Second, to make the trip on a motorcycle. And finally to share things she hadn't shared with anyone. Could she take that final step? To let God back into her life? She was afraid to fail. Fail to live up to the expectations of God, the church and herself. And Clay.

While her mind buzzed with all the reasons not to fall in love with Clay, he slowed the bike. She glanced toward the river. The golden foliage reflected in the water made an incredible picture. As she marveled at the magnificent sight, he drove off the main highway and stopped at a viewing area near the Box Canyon Dam.

Removing his helmet, he turned to her. "I thought you might like to see the bridge and the excursion train from here." He glanced at his watch. "The train should be along any minute now."

Beth stared at the bridge. Why did he have to stop? Now they would have to talk again. Conversation that she didn't want to have. That was the only good thing about making this trip on a motorcycle. She didn't have to make small talk. She had already spilled her guts to Clay this afternoon. She didn't want any more time for revelations.

Standing beside her, he put an arm around her shoulders and drew her close. "Great view, huh?"

"Yeah."

"Makes you really appreciate God's creation."

"Yeah."

He turned so they were facing each other. His gray eyes gazed directly into hers. "You don't want to talk, do you?"

"No." She wanted to look away but found she couldn't.

He gathered her into his arms. "Oh, Beth. I never dreamed when I came to the sleepy little town of Pinecrest that I would find a woman who made me want to stay."

Not wanting to look into his eyes, she tightened her arms around his waist and laid her head against his chest. His heartbeat pounded a steady rhythm. She swallowed a lump in her throat. "Don't say that."

"Why?"

"Because I know you'll leave, and you won't come back."

"Yes, I have to leave, but I'd come back if you gave me a reason to."

Shaking her head, she tried to rid her mind of any reason for him to return. She was only setting herself up for disappointment if she let that thought linger. "We can't change who we are and what we want."

"Yes, we can. You've already changed me."

She pushed her way out of his embrace and walked to the other side of the viewing area. She turned and looked back at him. "I'm not going to change. I'll always do something wrong."

"Beth, please don't run away." He strode to her and gathered her into his arms again. This time he kissed her.

She drank in the taste of him. It mingled with his scent, the smell of leather and pine forest. Her heart soared like the osprey flying high above the river and forested hillsides. The kiss took her higher and higher. She didn't want to come down. She wanted to stay suspended, on the mountaintop, away from all the things that could separate them.

When the kiss ended, he held her close. "Think about what I've said. I want a relationship with you, but I can't see that happening if—"

"If I don't return to God." Shaking her head, she pulled herself from his embrace. "I'm sorry. I can't do that. We just have to say good-bye."

He gently grabbed her shoulders. "Beth, I'm not just going to say good-bye. I'm not giving up on you."

Chapter Twelve

Humming a little tune, Beth hurried to get ready for her last dinner with Clay. Mere weeks ago the thought of having Clay gone hadn't bothered her. At least, not much. She had told herself that she wasn't interested in him and that he couldn't possibly be interested in her. Now she knew he was, but what good was that when he was leaving in a few days? How could they ever overcome the obstacles that separated them? The words *work and faith* whispered through her mind. But she wouldn't think about those things tonight. This was their chance to have a private farewell. Not the big fuss that Jillian had planned for tomorrow night.

She thought about Clay and Max and the companionship between them. How was Max going to deal with Clay's leaving?

While she waited for Clay to arrive, she grabbed a trash bag and went to empty the wastebaskets in the bath and bedrooms. She went into Max's room and picked up the basket from under his desk. It was stuffed full of papers. Turning it upside down, she dumped it into the bag. As she started to set it down, she noticed something sticking to the bottom of the basket. When she reached for it, her heart nearly stopped.

She didn't want to believe what she saw. No. It couldn't be what she thought. Her stomach lurching, she looked closer. She couldn't deny what lay there. Sinking to the bed, she stared at the wastebasket. Her worst fear had been realized.

What was going on with Max? Only weeks ago he had proclaimed his acceptance of Jesus as his savior. He had been all preachy with her and bugged her to renew her own faith. So what was she to make of the condom wrapper staring back at her?

A sob escaped. She swallowed hard as a tear flowed down her cheek. Was Max turning out to be like his father? Two-faced? Lying? And maybe getting some girl pregnant?

Brittany? Beth didn't want to believe that, either. The girl seemed so levelheaded. But maybe that was how everyone had viewed Jillian's nephew and his girlfriend.

Getting up from the bed, she let the wastebasket fall to the floor. She wiped a hand across her face as she headed for the kitchen. How could this be happening? How long had it been going on? And what about those abstinence lessons Sam and Clay had touted? The questions swirled in her mind while a sickening sensation filled her gut and tears ran down her cheeks.

When she entered the kitchen, a knock sounded on the door. She glanced up. Clay opened the door and stepped inside. She had no time to hide her tears.

"Beth, what's wrong?"

She shook her head, and he pulled her into his arms. They sheltered her. She laid her head on his chest and let the warmth of his embrace subdue the problems assailing her. How was she going to say good-bye to this man? What would he say when he found out about Max? Her troubles spelled doom for the quiet dinner they had planned. Not wanting to look at him, she let him hold her tightly. But she had to tell him something. She blinked back tears. "It's Max."

"Has something happened to him?"

How could she explain? Should she show Clay what she had found, or was this something she needed to talk to Max about first? She sighed and pulled herself from his embrace. "No, nothing has happened to him. At least not yet."

"What do you mean?"

"I'm afraid he's involved in some destructive behavior."

Shaking his head, Clay frowned. "What kind?"

"I'd rather not speculate about it now. I need to talk with Max first."

"When do you expect him home?"

"About ten. He went over to Brittany's to study." Beth wondered whether she had been too trusting, accepting everything Max had told her. She should've verified that Brittany's parents would be home. Had she been thinking so much about being with Clay that she had failed to be a vigilant parent?

"Are you going to talk then?"

"I need to talk to him now." Closing her eyes, Beth wanted to block out the image of the condom wrapper. But it kept creeping back into her mind. She had to call now. She'd never have any peace if she didn't. Opening her eyes, she looked at Clay. "This is going to ruin our evening. I'm so sorry."

"Not necessarily." His serious expression broke her heart.

"But I can't think of anything else. I'll be terrible company. I have to talk with Max now." She marched across the kitchen and started to pick up the phone.

Clay followed. Covering her hand with his, he stopped her. "Wait a minute, and think about what you're doing."

"I know what I'm doing. I'm checking to see whether Max told me the truth." She frowned at Clay.

"So you're saying maybe Max has lied to you?"

"I'm not sure."

"May I make a suggestion?"

"Why?" Didn't he understand that Max was her responsibility? Or was Clay afraid his church stuff hadn't rubbed off on Max as he'd thought it would?

"So you won't rush to judgment."

"I'm not." Beth shook her head. "I'm calling because I can't enjoy my evening until I talk with Max."

Clay placed his hands on her shoulders. "I don't think Max would lie to you."

"I hope you're right." Beth punched in the Gormans' number. When Lori answered, Beth breathed a momentary sigh of relief. At least a parent was at home. "Hi, Lori. This is Beth. Max told me he was studying with Brittany."

"Yes, they both have their noses in a book." Lori chuckled.

"He needs to come home now."

"Is there a problem?"

"No, he just needs to come home." Beth hoped Lori wouldn't press further about the situation. What would this woman do if she knew there was a possibility that her daughter was sexually active with Max? Panic filled her mind at the thought.

"I'll send him home immediately."

Knowing Max was actually where he said he would be lifted Beth's spirits a little. She looked at Clay, who flashed her a questioning glance. She gave him a thumbs-up, and he smiled. It melted her heart. "Yeah, that'll be fine. Thanks so much, Lori."

Clay took the phone from her and hung it up. "Maybe you're worrying for nothing."

Pressing her lips together, Beth shook her head. "No. Something's not right, and I'm getting to the bottom of it. Max is coming home."

"I wish you'd share, so I could help you."

"I know, but this is something between Max and me. If I think I need your input later, I'll talk to you."

Clay took her hands in his. "I hate having to leave just when—"

"When you just about have me convinced that I can trust God?"

"Yeah, that. But there's more."

"More what?"

"You and me, Beth."

Her heart aching, she shook her head. "There can't be a you and me when you'll be somewhere else."

"I can always come back to see you."

"What good is a weekend here and there, especially when I'll be in class on Saturday?"

"There are phone calls and e-mail."

"And how do I get e-mail without a computer? As it is, I have to do my class papers at the college library."

"That's something I wanted to discuss with you tonight. I'm going to leave my laptop here for you and Max to use."

"What will you use?"

"The new one I'm planning to buy."

"More than distance stands between us."

"Are you talking about your faith in God?"

"Yes, that's the biggest obstacle."

"But you know you're almost persuaded."

"Almost persuaded?" Beth whispered the words from a song in the hymnal. "'Sad, sad that bitter wail, Almost, but lost.'" Lost. That's what she was. Having turned her back on God years ago, wasn't she beyond redemption now?

"God's waiting for you. I want to help you find your way back to Him."

Beth saw Max ride up on his bike, rescuing her from further discussion about God. "Max is here."

"Think about what I've said. We can work something out. I'll call you in a little while." Clay gave Beth a kiss on the cheek and ducked out the back door.

Beth met Max as he walked in the front door. "Max, please have a seat."

"What for?" A puzzled expression on his face, he shrugged out of his jacket. "Is something wrong?"

"You tell me." She produced the wastebasket from behind her back and held it so he could see inside. "Can you explain what that is doing in there?"

His face went white. Something flickered across his eyes. Fear? Worry? Embarrassment? Then he shook his head. "I don't know where that came from."

"Well, it certainly isn't mine. It was in *your* waste-basket in *your* room, so seems to me it belongs to you."

He continued to shake his head. "No, Mom, you gotta believe me. It's not mine."

"Then how did it get there?"

He dropped his gaze. "I don't know."

He wouldn't meet her eyes. Beth wanted to die inside. He wasn't telling her the truth. She could read it in his body language. "You know something about this. And I want an answer. Have you and Brittany been sexually active?"

Jumping up, he shook his head. "No! We're just friends." His brow wrinkled with concern. "You gotta believe me. What can I do to convince you?"

"Tell me the truth." Beth stared at her son.

"I am."

"Not completely." Beth shook her head. "There's something you're not telling me."

"I don't know anything about that condom." Max grabbed his jacket and stomped to the door. "I'm not going to talk to someone who calls me a liar."

"Don't you dare leave, young man."

"You can't stop me." He slammed out of the house.

Beth ran after him, but he sprinted away into the night. She'd never catch up to him. Where was he going? She bit her lip as tears filled her eyes. He had seemed so adamant that the condom wasn't his. Had he been telling the truth? But where had it come from? Nothing made sense.

Shivering, she continued to stand on the sidewalk as she faced the darkness. Had she been too harsh with Max? What should she do? She turned toward the house. Could she talk with Clay? She didn't see any lights in his apartment. He wasn't home. Why had she insisted on talking with Max alone? Maybe he wouldn't have run off if Clay had been there to help. Why did she always make the wrong choice?

Clay glanced around the office one last time. In less than two days he'd be gone. When he drove out of town on Sunday afternoon, he'd leave three things behind. His motorcycle, his laptop and his heart. He hated leaving his bike, but he needed a car while he was in Seattle. But leaving Beth and Max bothered him more than anything. The thought made him ache inside. This whole falling-in-love thing hurt.

He couldn't stay, and she couldn't go. And more important than that was Beth's opposition to church and God. She couldn't let go of the hurts from the past. He saw no way to help her overcome that obstacle to faith. She had to do that on her own. Until she did, he had to say good-bye. Besides, she didn't care about him the way he cared about her.

He had hoped to talk with her tonight, but some episode with Max had blown the evening completely.

While Clay dumped his meager belongings into a box, his cell phone rang. It had to be Beth, but when he looked at the display screen it read, *Unknown call.* Who could it be? "Clay Reynolds."

"Clay?" Max's muffled voice came through the receiver.

"Max?" There was silence. "Max, are you okay?"

"I need your help." Desperation sounded in Max's voice.

An uneasy feeling settled in Clay's chest. "How can I help?"

"I need to talk. Can you meet me at the Pinecrest Café?"

"Sure. I'll be there in five minutes."

On the drive to the café, Clay wondered whether he should call Beth or talk to Max first. Clay prayed for wisdom. What had happened between Beth and Max? Had Max gotten into some kind of trouble again? Clay didn't want to believe it, but sometimes peer pressure got the best of kids.

Clay walked into the nearly empty café. One man sat at the counter. Near the door two couples occupied booths with bright red vinyl upholstery. Max sat at the back in one of the booths. A drink and a plate of fries sat on the table. Clay slid into the seat across from the teen.

"What's going on?"

Max didn't say anything. He dipped fries into the ketchup and shoveled them into his mouth instead. His gaze didn't meet Clay's.

Speculation ran wild as Clay waited. The waitress appeared, and he ordered a cola.

After the waitress left, Max looked up and leaned forward. "My mom thinks Brittany and I are sexually active."

The whispered words punched Clay in the gut. Probably nothing could upset Beth more. Well, Max certainly knew how to get to the point. "Are you?"

"No, but she wouldn't believe me. She said I was lying."

Clay raised his eyebrows. "She said that? She must have a good reason. Would you like to explain?"

Not meeting Clay's gaze, Max twirled a fry through the ketchup and continued to talk barely above a whisper. "She found a condom wrapper in the wastebasket in my room. But I've never even bought a condom."

Clay swallowed a lump in his throat. Could he believe Max? Everything he had seen from the boy in the past few weeks told him he could. "Then how do you suppose it got there?"

Max sighed. "I think I know."

"Did you explain that to your mom?"

"No. I couldn't."

"Why not?"

Max doodled with the fry again. "Because I just couldn't tell her about the party."

"The party?"

"Yeah. There was a party at our house while you guys were on that retreat."

Clay felt sick inside. So Max had been involved in another unsupervised party, probably with drinking and sex, if the condom was any indication. "So how did this party come about?"

"It wasn't my idea." Max glanced up. "They blackmailed me."

"Who is 'they'?"

"Ryan and that bunch who had the party where I got drunk."

"So what was the blackmail?"

"They found out that you guys were going to be gone. They cornered me after the game on Friday. They told me I had to let them have a party at my place on Saturday night or they would tell Coach about the night I got drunk and get me kicked off the team."

"Why didn't you tell someone?"

"You guys were gone." Max hung his head. "And Ryan is a big suck-up. Coach believes everything he says. Ryan had me fooled, too. I thought he was my friend."

"Were you at the party?"

"For a while, but I didn't drink. Honest. I'm done with that stuff. I know better now. I just wanted to make sure they didn't trash the place. I kept warning them not to mess anything up." Max took a gulp of his drink. "I couldn't get them to leave before I had to show up at the Lawsons, where I was staying. I just prayed they wouldn't ruin any of Mom's stuff."

"And did they?"

Max shook his head. "No, but they left a mess. I spent most of Sunday afternoon cleaning up. I was worried sick you guys would get home before I was done."

"So you thought you had pulled it off?"

"I wasn't trying to pull anything off. I just didn't want to get kicked off the team." Irritation colored Max's words.

"What makes you think Ryan won't blackmail you again?"

"You think that could happen?" Max's eyes opened wide.

"Possibly."

"What am I going to do?"

"You have one choice." Clay sighed. "You've got to tell your mom the truth."

"I can't."

"You don't have a choice."

"She's already mad at me because I ran out on her. Now she's really gonna be mad. Mad enough to ground me for the rest of my life. Will you help me?"

"You ran out on her tonight?"

"She wouldn't believe me."

"That was no excuse to run out on your mom."

"Well, I did." Max frowned.

Bowing his head, Clay rubbed his forehead. "Pay your bill. Then we'll go."

On the ride back to the house, Clay prayed that somehow this would work out for good. God's promise from the Scripture said, *In all things God works for the good of those who love him.* Sometimes it was so hard to see how God was going to make good out of certain situations.

When Clay pulled his new car into the garage, Max asked him, "Will you talk to her?"

"What would you want me to say?"

Max shrugged. "That I'm telling the truth?"

"But you haven't told her the whole truth." Clay headed toward the house.

Max hurried to follow. "But she doesn't believe any of it."

"She probably will once you tell her everything."

"I have to do that?"

"Yep. I'll go with you, but you do the talking."

Clay stood behind Max as he slowly opened the back door leading into the kitchen.

"Mom?" Max called softly.

There was no answer. He walked into the house. Clay stayed close behind. Max stopped in the living room. Beth's bedroom door was closed.

Max went over and tapped on the door. "Mom, are you in there?" He waited a minute. There was no response. "Mom, I'm sorry about earlier. Mom—"

The door opened, and Beth stepped past Max into the living room. Even her glasses didn't hide red eyes that swam with disappointment. Red tinged the tip of her nose. She looked at Clay, then at Max. "I don't even know what to say to you. Do you have an explanation for your behavior?"

Max glanced back at Clay as if he thought Clay would rescue him at the last moment. Clay wanted to rescue both of them. If he could just take Beth into his arms and make the hurt go away. But that wasn't going to happen.

Staring at Max, Clay nodded in Beth's direction. "She's waiting for an explanation."

Beth stood there with her arms crossed and expectation written on her face. "Yes, I am."

Max's Adam's apple bobbed as he turned to his mother. "I don't know where to start."

"How about starting with that condom wrapper? How did it get into your trash?"

"I'm not sure." Max shrugged.

"That's your explanation?" Beth narrowed her gaze.

"No." Max paused and started pacing, then stopped and faced his mother again. "I let some guys have a party here while you were gone. One of them must have used my room. I couldn't keep track of all the people in the house," he blurted.

Beth looked horrified. "An unsupervised party? Here? What else was going on at this party besides people having sex in your room?"

"Drinking and stuff."

Arms still crossed, Beth shook her head. "I don't even want to ask about the 'stuff.' Why would you do such a thing?"

Max grimaced and turned to Clay one more time.

Clay wished he could help the kid out of this mess,

but Max had to face the consequences of his actions. Maybe that's what he should have helped the boy do from the beginning. Now Beth would hear the disappointing truth anyway. "Go ahead. Tell her."

While Clay listened, Max told Beth about getting drunk and how Ryan and his friends had blackmailed him into having the party.

After Max finished talking, Beth looked at Clay. Her eyes flashed with disillusionment. Then she turned back to Max. "I can't even begin to tell you how disappointed I am in your behavior." The calm in her voice belied the anger written on her face. "I'll have to consider your punishment, but right now go to your room and stay there until I tell you to come out."

"Mom, please...I'm sorry."

Beth pointed toward his bedroom door. "Just go to your room."

Max shuffled toward his room and disappeared inside.

When the door shut, Beth turned on Clay. The anger he had seen earlier was now directed at him. "You knew about this?"

"Not about this latest party, but I knew he got drunk after his first football game."

"And you didn't tell me?" The words came out in a harsh whisper.

Feeling as called on the carpet as Max had been, Clay wished he had told Beth about her son's misbehavior from the beginning. He had thought he was doing the right thing. But he still had a lot to learn. Now Clay had to pay the consequences for his actions, too. "That's right. I thought I was doing the best thing at the time."

She closed her eyes and pressed her fingers to her forehead as if to calm herself. Silence filled the room. Finally opening her eyes, she glared at him. "I can't begin to tell you how angry I am at Max *and* at you."

Clay shook his head. "Maybe I should have told you."

"Maybe? Maybe?" Her voice rose a pitch with each word. "You covered for him. That was dishonest. You spout all this Christianity to me, but you…you can't even tell the truth."

"I didn't lie. But I made a mistake in not telling you."

"You certainly did." Her voice calm again, she gave him a stare. "Please leave."

"Beth, I was wrong. Can't you forgive me?"

Shaking her head, she pushed at her glasses. "I shared so much with you. Things I've not talked about with anyone in years. And you couldn't tell me the truth about my own son. I don't want to see or talk to you again." Her mouth formed a grim line. She walked to the front door and opened it. "Please leave."

"Beth—"

"Just leave."

Releasing a ragged breath, Clay stepped outside. The door closed behind him with a thud. When he turned to look back, Beth had already shut off the light. Clay's heart ached as he dragged himself to the stairs at the back of the house. With each step up to his apartment he berated his foolishness in his dealings with Max.

Tonight Clay had planned to tell Beth he loved her. Now she wouldn't even talk to him. He was leaving, and his plans lay in shambles. Stopping for a moment at the top of the stairs, he stared at the sky. Clouds raced across the moon. A chilly wind rattled the bare branches of the row of trees separating the backyard from the neighbor's. Winter was in the air, sending a shiver through Clay's body. But the thought of never seeing Beth again sent a chill through his heart. How could he ever deal with that? He bowed his head. *Lord, help me to understand what You want. Help me to see Your plan.*

Chapter Thirteen

Beth stood in the living room in the dark. The only illumination came from the streetlamp shining through the sheer curtains on the front window. She should have known better than to think she could have a relationship with Clay. She had let her foolish heart fall in love again with a man who had turned out to be less than trustworthy. She wanted to curl up in a ball and cry. Shut out the whole world and make the hurt go away. But she had a son to deal with.

What was she going to do with Max? Ground him until he finished high school? That would be stupid. Despite the negative thoughts she had had about her parents over the years, she was beginning to see the difficulties they had faced in dealing with her. They could have done a better job, but she hadn't made it easy. They had been too strict, and she had been too rebellious.

In some ways she had looked at Clay as an ally in dealing with Max. Now Clay had let her down, too. She had no one to count on but herself. And she didn't know what to do. Leaning against the curio cabinets, she stared at Max's door in the dim light. In the quiet, she heard Clay enter his apartment upstairs. The sound of his door closing seemed to press on her heart and squeeze the life out of it.

Taking a deep breath, she approached Max's room. A light shining under the door sent a beam onto the dining-room floor. Beth knocked. "Max, I'd like to talk to you now."

A shuffling sound came from the other side of the door. It opened wide. Max stood in the doorway. He hung his head, but he couldn't hide the fact that he'd been crying. Her big six-foot son was still a kid after all. Her heart turned to mush. He was on the verge of adulthood but not there yet. She wanted so badly to reach out and hug him, but she had to dish out his punishment before she weakened.

"Come out to the living room." She turned on a light as she led the way. She motioned to the couch. "Have a seat."

Max settled on the couch, his head lowered. "So what's my punishment?"

She just wanted to gather him into her arms and tell him everything was going to be okay. But he had to suffer some consequences for his behavior. If only she had the wisdom to do the right thing. "Look at me, Max."

He raised his head. His eyes projected worry as his Adam's apple bobbed. "Just tell me what it is."

"I wish I didn't have to do this, but I'm going to ground you until Thanksgiving."

"What does that mean, exactly?"

"Well, you'll be expected to come home immediately after school. No going out on the weekends. No TV. No friends over to the house. And instead of my paying half the cost of your driving lessons, you get to pay for the entire thing. So that means no permit until you've earned the money."

"How am I supposed to earn the money if I can't go out? I've already lined up some jobs. People are expecting me."

"You'll give me a schedule of your jobs. When you get to the job, you explain to the people about being grounded and tell them they need to let me know when you arrive and when you leave."

"But you're in class during some of that time. How's that going to work?"

Beth sighed. "I'll get Kim to make sure you're where you say you are."

"Oh, swell, now everyone's gonna know I'm in trouble."

"Watch your mouth. You're treading a thin line here."

"Sorry." He lowered his gaze. "What about church?"

Church hadn't been on her radar screen. What good had church been? It hadn't kept him out of trouble. What should she do about that? If she didn't let him go, would that be pushing things too far? Her parents had pushed her too far. Funny. Her parents had saturated her with church stuff, and she had rebelled. Now her son wanted to go to church. Would he rebel if she didn't let him? "Okay, here's the deal with church. You can go on Sunday mornings and come directly home."

"But, Mom, I'm supposed to be part of the program the Sunday after Thanksgiving. I have to rehearse."

"What are you supposed to do in this program?"

He hung his head again. "I was going to be in one of the skits and give a short lesson."

"You mean like a sermon?"

"If that's what you want to call it."

"And you feel right about doing that after the way you've behaved?"

"It's something I promised to do." He looked up. "Everyone makes mistakes."

Beth instantly sympathized with that. She had made plenty of mistakes herself. And sometimes even wrong choices could turn out okay. Getting involved with Max's dad had been a wrong choice, but in the end it had turned her life around. She'd had to grow up and take responsibility for herself and a new young life. Despite their trouble now, having Max was the best thing that had ever happened. Would Max's mistakes help him turn away from the wrong friends? How should she handle this?

"Okay, since you've already promised, I want you to make an appointment for us to talk with Sam, since he's the youth pastor."

"Mom!" Max wailed. "Why don't I just take out an ad in the local paper or put it up on a billboard that I messed up?"

"It's not that bad. You're just grounded."

"And what about Clay's going-away party?"

Another thing she hadn't thought about. She definitely didn't want to go to Clay's party now, but if she refused, she would face questions she didn't want to answer. Better to go and put on a happy face than try to explain why she wouldn't be there. One last night, and he would be gone. Gone forever. Out of her life. Good riddance, right? But if that was the case, why did she feel so awful?

"I'm not real happy with Clay right now, either, but we'll go to the party together for a little while."

Standing, Max looked down at her. "I know you've got good reason to be unhappy with both of us, but I want you to know Clay has helped me a lot. He's made a big difference in my life. Despite that party, he helped steer me away from a bad crowd. I wish you'd believe that."

Beth looked up at her beloved son. She hated to punish him at all, but as his parent, she had to establish discipline. She knew he was a good boy, but she wanted him to grow up to be a good *man*. "I think you can testify to that fact by the way you behave during the time you're grounded."

"I'm going to show you what it means to follow Jesus, Mom. I'll prove to you that I'm on the right path now."

"We'll see."

Beth stood near a window in Jillian and Sam's living room and balanced a plate of hors d'oeuvres in her hand. The laughter and pleasant conversation around her didn't brighten her mood. Despite the dusting of snow on the ground and trees outside, the house was warm and inviting as a fire roared in the huge hearth. But Beth's heart was cold. Nothing could warm it.

Dozens of people had come to say good-bye to Clay. She intended to make an appearance and then her excuses to leave. She watched Max as he joined in conversation and laughter with several teens, including Brittany. Surprisingly, Max was dealing with his punishment without complaining. He had provided her with his list of jobs and had already talked with Sam about the teen program.

Clay talked and laughed with a group of guys in the kitchen. Other than an initial hello and a questioning glance, he hadn't said a word to her the whole evening. Turning away, she stared at the reflection of the fire in the nearby window. Everything seemed to be going well. Why was she so miserable?

"I'd like to talk to you for a minute."

Beth nearly jumped at the sound of Clay's voice, but she didn't turn around. "Do we have anything to talk about?"

"I want to continue a conversation we started last night but never finished."

"If we didn't finish it, then I didn't want to. And I still don't."

"I know you don't, but we have some unfinished business. So hear me out."

With a sigh, Beth crossed her arms. "All right. Say what you've got to say."

"It's about the computer. I told Max he could have it. You can use it, too. For your papers. Then you won't have to spend so much time at the library. You can do your papers at home." The words tumbled from his mouth as if he was afraid she wouldn't let him finish.

"Okay. Thank you for letting Max have the computer. But you know that your generous gift doesn't change the fact that you aided my son in deceiving me."

"And I said I was wrong."

"Let's just leave it at that, then. No more discussion."

"Hey, you two. Just the people I was looking for." Kim's voice made Beth turn.

Beth frowned. "Why?"

"You remember that day at the school festival when

Clay agreed that if you dunked him in the tank, you could cut his hair?" Kim grinned. "We've got everything ready in the other room, so you can have the pleasure of cutting off that ponytail."

Beth wanted to run somewhere and hide. Just what she didn't need. An all-too-intimate moment with Clay. "That's okay. I'd forgotten all about that. He probably wants a barber to cut it."

"Oh, no. We want to see you do it. Don't spoil our fun." Kim started to drag Beth toward the kitchen. "Come on. Everyone's waiting."

"I don't know how to cut hair. Why don't you do it?" Beth glanced at Clay. Was he in on this, or was he just as surprised as she was?

"You don't need to give him a real haircut. You just cut the ponytail off. Then Ray's going to finish the job. He's a barber." Kim grabbed Clay's arm and escorted him to a chair in the middle of the kitchen.

Clay still hadn't said a word. What was he thinking? His expression gave her no clue. She had waited too long to leave the party. Now she couldn't escape. She'd have to go along with this. "All right. What do I need to do?"

As Clay sat on the chair, teasing remarks came from the crowd gathered around the kitchen. He laughed. "I'm glad you guys are having so much fun at my expense."

"Put this on him." Kim handed Beth a cape. "Ray brought it from his shop."

Beth grabbed the cape, slung it across Clay's chest and used the Velcro to close it around his neck. Her hands shook as they brushed his skin. "Now what?"

"Take these and cut away." Kim handed her a pair of scissors.

"Hey, before you start, we have some procedures to follow here. Okay?" Clay turned and looked at Beth.

Taking the scissors, Beth smiled. "Okay, shoot."

Clay held up a hand. "We have to make sure you cut the hair so it's at least ten inches long."

"Got the tape measure right here." Kim stepped up beside Clay's chair and measured his ponytail. She turned to Beth. "Looks like you can cut it just above the elastic."

Clay held up a hand again. "One more thing. When you cut it, hold on to it so it doesn't fall on the floor. Then put it into a plastic bag."

Kim snatched a bag from a nearby box on the counter and held it close to Beth. "Check. Go ahead and cut, Beth. I'll hold the bag right here, and you can pop the hair in as soon as you cut it."

"Yeah, go ahead before he thinks of something else to keep those scissors at bay. I think he's gotten too attached to that hair," someone in the crowd teased.

Carefully waving the scissors like a wand, Beth decided she was having fun after all. Cutting Clay's hair was almost symbolic of cutting him out of her life. She was going to enjoy this. "All right. Everyone ready?"

A loud chorus of yeses sounded throughout the kitchen.

With one swift click of the scissors, Clay's ponytail came off into Beth's hand. She deposited it into the bag and held it up to a round of applause. Smiling, she took a bow. Then she glanced at Clay. He reminded her of a the little Dutch boy, with dark rather than blond hair.

He grinned. Her heart fluttered, and she was lost all over again. She needed to get out of here before his presence undid her resolve to cut him out of her life completely. What was wrong with her? He had betrayed her trust. How could her silly heart forget?

She handed him the bag containing the hair, then swiftly turned to Kim to give her the scissors.

As Kim took them, Beth melted into the crowd. She searched for Max. He stood off to one side with Brittany, watching Clay and the barber. Beth scooted through the group until she reached Max.

Leaning close, she whispered, "Max, we need to go."

He looked her way with a pleading expression. "Can't we wait until Ray finishes cutting Clay's hair?"

"Why do you have to watch a haircut?"

"It's part of the fun."

"Well, as I recall, you're grounded. So the fun's over." Beth motioned toward the door. "Say good-bye to your friends, and head for the car. I'm going to let Jillian know we're leaving. I expect to see you in the car when I get there."

Scowling, Max didn't say a word as he followed her toward the front hall, where they got their coats from the closet. Max shrugged into his jacket and stomped out the front door.

Coat in hand, Beth tiptoed up to Jillian. "Hey, Jillian, thanks for the great party. Sorry I can't stay longer, but I have studying to do."

"Do you have to rush off? Clay still hasn't opened his gift."

Beth nodded. "Max is already in the car."

"Well, I'm glad you got to come for a little while and that you were here to cut Clay's hair. We got a chuckle out of that." Jillian gave Beth a hug. "Drive safely back to town."

"I will. Thanks again." Beth opened the door and stepped onto the porch.

"Beth, why are you leaving so soon?" Kim poked her head out the door.

"Gotta study."

Despite the cold evening, Kim came outside without her coat. "I can't believe you're leaving without saying good-bye to Clay."

"We've said our good-byes. I don't want to prolong it."

"But I thought—"

"You thought wrong. I know you hoped your matchmaking would work out, but it didn't. Please just let it go. Some things are better left alone." Beth turned and raced to the car as tears spilled down her cheeks. She brushed the tears away with her coat sleeve. She wouldn't let Max know she had been crying.

Clay leaned back in his chair and drank in the laughter and conversation emanating from the fourteen family members crammed around the table in his mother's dining room. The aroma of his mother's fabulous cooking permeated the air. A traditional Thanksgiving feast filled his plate. It was good to be home to share this day with his brothers, Grady and Trent, and his sister, Leslie, and their families, as well as his mom. It almost made up for not being with Beth and Max.

"This turkey is great, Mom." Thankful for his wonderful family, Clay took another bite.

"I'm glad you like it. I know you were doing good deeds by helping at a soup kitchen the past few years, but I sure enjoy having you here for Thanksgiving." His mother picked up the bowl of mashed potatoes and passed it to him. "Have some more potatoes."

Clay took the bowl. "This is why I only do this every few years. You're going to make me fat."

"You could use some meat on those bones. I know you've lost weight since I saw you last. And I'm certainly glad you finally cut that hair."

"Must be his own awful cooking that took off the pounds." Trent, the younger of Clay's two older brothers, poked him playfully in the arm.

"Probably." Clay didn't argue. He had lost weight but not because of his own admittedly bad cooking. Since leaving Pinecrest he had buried himself in his consulting job, hoping it would keep him from thinking about Beth. And Max. He just didn't bother to eat sometimes. He had lost his appetite. Living in the big city suddenly felt lonely. Even the church he attended made him lonely, because he knew he wouldn't be there long enough to form any friendships. He'd soon be moving on to his next project. He missed the church in Pinecrest. He was tired of his temporary life.

He didn't want to think about Beth and Max now, but he couldn't help wondering how they were enjoying their Thanksgiving with the Lawsons. He had hoped to share this day with them, but Beth had not forgiven him for his interference in her family. He prayed that she would, but he knew being a single parent made her ferociously defensive about her son. And no wonder. He had been wrong to butt in.

"Do you want pie now or later?" His mother's question brought Clay's thoughts back to his own family.

"Definitely later." He patted his stomach.

"I suppose you boys are going to watch football all afternoon and leave the cleanup to Leslie and me." Clay's mother looked across the table at him.

"Never, Mom." Clay chuckled. "We'll all help. Then you can watch football with us."

She waved a hand at him. "No football for me."

Clay joined his siblings and the grandkids as they pitched in to clear the table. Soon they had the dishwasher loaded and the last pan washed. Clay hung his dishtowel on the rack and then joined his brothers in front of the TV.

At halftime Grady stood up and stretched. "Well, gotta take Amanda and Kelsey over to see the other set of grandparents." He glanced at Clay. "We'll get together again before you leave. I'll give you a call."

Clay stood. "Sure. Let me give those nieces of mine another hug before you take off."

After following Grady to the front door, Clay said his good-byes and grabbed a piece of pie on his way back to the family room. While he watched the rest of the game, he couldn't help thinking about Max. What Clay wouldn't give to be watching the game with that kid and his mom. Was there any possibility that Clay could make amends by Christmastime? What chance was there when he was so far away and Beth wouldn't talk to him even for a minute?

"Not watching the game? You look a thousand miles away." Trent's voice broke through the cloud of Clay's worry.

Clay laughed halfheartedly. "Yeah. That's about the distance."

"Does this have something to do with the picture of a woman you have on your computer?"

"How did you see that?"

"I was walking by when you logged on earlier today."
Trent flashed Clay a speculative glance. "Who is she?"

Did he really want to explain? He might as well, or
the topic would come up again and again. "She was my
downstairs neighbor in Pinecrest."

"That doesn't exactly explain why you have her
picture on your log-in screen."

"No, I guess it doesn't. Are you sure you want to hear
the story?"

"Absolutely, little brother."

Clay gave Trent a short rendition of his time in Pinecrest. Clay explained how he had met Beth and how she
had turned his world completely around. "I think I was
a goner from the moment I looked into those blue eyes.
And besides that, she's got a great kid. But she can't get
over a lot of hurt from her past."

"I can't believe you would even consider living in a
small town again. When you left here, you vowed never
to be stuck in a 'one-horse town' again."

Clay shook his head. "I know. I can't believe it either.
Coming home has really opened my eyes, too."

"How?"

"After I went with Mom and Amanda to Kelsey's
basketball practice, we went out to eat. Everywhere we
went, people stopped to say hello. It reminded me of
being in Pinecrest. How the people there care about one
another. When I was a kid, I felt stifled by everyone's
knowing my business."

"That's because you were always getting into trouble."

"Don't I know it." Clay nodded. "But working in the
city again has shown me that I don't want to be alone
in a crowd anymore. I thought that's what I wanted. I

thought all my traveling was great until I went to Pinecrest and found out how wonderful a settled life can be. Now I realize it's not so much where you live as being with the people you love."

"Are you saying you're in love with Beth?"

"Yes. I didn't want to fall in love with her, because she doesn't share my faith, but I did anyway."

"Well, what do you plan to do about it?"

"I don't know." Clay shrugged. "Pray. That's all I can do. I've thought a lot about her being estranged from her parents. Maybe if she reconciled with them, she could rediscover her faith."

"What do you know about her parents?"

"They lived in Ohio when Beth left home."

"Do they still live there?"

"I don't have a clue," Clay replied, shaking his head. "That was over fifteen years ago."

"Wow. Fifteen years without speaking to her parents. I can't imagine."

"Me neither. Even with the problems Dad and I had, we still spoke to each other."

Trent chuckled. "Yeah. Mostly while he was bailing you out of some kind of trouble."

"That's true, but at least in the end Dad and I came to an understanding. We forgave each other." Clay nodded. "I want that for Beth."

"How do you plan to accomplish that?"

"What do you think about trying to find her parents?"

"Could be touchy."

"Yeah, but I've been praying about that, too. I figure if the Lord wants me to find Beth's parents, I will. If He doesn't, I won't."

"I'll be praying for you and Beth."

"Thanks."

Frowning, Trent shook his head. "Beth isn't the only one we need to pray for. Grady could use our prayers. He hasn't been right since Nina's death. He's drifted completely away from the church. None of us can talk to him."

"I didn't realize Grady had stopped going to church."

"Yeah. Maybe you should talk to him."

Clay wrinkled his brow. "And you think he'll listen to his *little* brother?"

"Maybe." Trent shrugged. "He can't go on blaming God for his wife's death. It's not just how it's affecting Grady. It's taking a toll on Amanda and Kelsey, too. He's become practically an absentee father. He always worked a lot, but now he spends almost every waking hour at the office. Mom, Nina's mother or the housekeeper takes care of the girls. I'm worried about them."

"That bad, huh?"

"Yeah, and the two grandmothers are enabling him to continue on this path."

"Have you talked to them?"

"It falls on deaf ears."

"Well, maybe I can talk with Grady when I ask him to recommend a good private detective, someone he uses for his cases."

"Great idea."

Chapter Fourteen

Clay stared at the piece of paper in his hand. An address and a phone number. In less than three weeks, Grady's private investigator had located Beth's parents. They still lived in Ohio in a small town near Dayton. Clay had flown into Dayton and rented a car. Strangely enough, as he drove into the Carlsons' little town, it reminded him of Pinecrest. He barely touched the gas pedal as he searched for the correct house on Elm Street. When he spied the address, he parked the car across the street from the gray-shingled house with white trim. The late-afternoon sun glinted off the glass in the storm door that protected a Christmas wreath.

Now that he was here, he wasn't sure what to do. Did he just go up to the house and ring the bell, or should he call first? What could he say to these people who hadn't spoken to their daughter in fifteen years? How would they react? Did he dare hope they would be happy to learn about their daughter?

With the questions rolling through his mind, he got

out of the car. Best to see the Carlsons in person. Taking a deep breath and squaring his shoulders, he started up the front walk. A cold wind rattled the bare branches of the trees surrounding the house. He shivered as he hesitated on the porch. *Lord, give me the right words as I speak with Beth's parents. Give her father a forgiving and accepting heart.*

His pulse racing, Clay punched the doorbell. He stood there for what seemed like an eternity. Finally the door opened. A slightly plump woman with short silver hair stood inside the storm door. Her blue eyes stared at him. Blue eyes like Beth's.

"Hello. My name is Clay Reynolds, and I'm looking for Sara and Allen Carlson."

The woman gave him a suspicious look and didn't open the storm door. "I'm Sara Carlson, but I'm not interested in buying anything."

"I'm not selling anything. I was hoping I could talk to you about your daughter, Beth."

The color drained from Sara's face as she opened the storm door about six inches. "How do you know her?"

"Honey, who's at the door?" a male voice called from somewhere in the house before Clay could answer.

Sara turned toward the voice. "Someone who knows Beth."

In a moment a man appeared behind Sara. He had thinning brown hair sprinkled with gray. From behind wire-framed glasses his hazel eyes peered at Clay. "You know our daughter?"

Clay nodded. "Yes, I was hoping I could speak to you about her."

"Sara, please let the man in."

She opened the door, and Clay stepped inside. He glanced around, taking in the small Christmas tree, twinkling with lights, situated in one corner of the living room. Then he looked back at the man.

"I'm Allen Carlson. And you are?"

"Clay Reynolds." Clay extended his hand.

With a firm grip, Allen shook Clay's hand. "Is Beth okay?"

Clay didn't know what to make of Allen's question. Did he really care after not speaking with her for years? "Yes, she's doing very well."

Relief flooded Allen's face. "I'm glad to hear it." Pausing, he appeared to be thinking about what he intended to say next as he reached for his wife's hand and brought her close. "Could you tell us how you know our daughter?"

Leaving out his romantic feelings for Beth, Clay gave the Carlsons a brief account of his time in Pinecrest. He wanted to get a better sense of their thoughts about her before he revealed any more. She didn't need a negative response from them. "I know the bad history between you and your daughter, but I was hoping you could find it in your hearts to forgive her."

"So this was your idea to find us? Not Beth's?" Allen asked.

Clay nodded. "I wasn't sure how Beth would react to the idea of finding you, besides not having the time or the means to search for you herself. I didn't know whether I could find you or how you would receive her if I did. So I've done this on my own."

Sara grabbed Clay's arm as tears welled in her eyes. "You are…this is an answer to our prayers."

"You've been praying for Beth?" Clay asked, surprised by her statement.

"Oh, yes." Sara looked at her husband.

Allen stepped forward and gestured toward the living room. "Let me take your coat, and we can talk."

Clay took off his coat and handed it to Allen and then followed Sara into the living room. As Clay headed toward the sofa, he noticed an oak wall unit. Framed pictures of Beth as a youngster occupied almost every shelf. Why would they display photographs of her and yet totally strike her from their lives? Could he ask without being rude? "Pictures of Beth?"

"Yes, these are all we have." With regret painting her words, Sara picked up one of the photos and handed it to Clay.

Clay studied the image. "She looks happy."

"She was such a good girl. Then it all just went wrong." Sara's voice cracked, and she glanced away. "Will she ever forgive us?"

Allen laid a hand on Sara's shoulder. "That's what we've been praying for, dear."

Looking at her husband, Sara squared her shoulders and nodded. "Yes, I have to believe our prayers have been answered." She turned back to Clay. "Please have a seat."

Clay sat on a floral-print love seat while Allen and Sara sat next to each other on the matching sofa. Again Allen held Sara's hand. Still wondering whether he had done the right thing to come here, Clay waited for Beth's parents to speak.

Allen leaned forward. "Is there any possibility that Beth would be willing to see us?"

"I have no idea," Clay replied, amazed at Allen's

request. What had brought about this change of heart? "I wanted to find you because I thought if she found peace with you, she might also turn her life back to God."

"That's what we want, too." Allen sighed and looked down at the floor. "I suppose you're wondering why we've never tried to contact her."

"Yes."

"For years we were under the impression Beth didn't want anything to do with us."

Clay frowned. "From what Beth told me, I thought it was the other way around."

"Yes, in the beginning we were embarrassed, angry. We had told her that Harkin boy was trouble, but she defied us and went with him anyway." Closing her eyes, Sara shook her head as misery covered her face. With a sigh, she opened her eyes and gazed at Clay. "I just thought it would be easier for all of us if she stayed with Violet until the baby was born and then give it up for adoption. But it seemed that whatever we said, she did the opposite."

"She defied us at every turn," Allen said. "There were a lot of bad feelings between us." Allen looked up at Clay. "And we didn't handle the situation well. We stopped communicating with her, but eventually we realized that wasn't right. We called at first, but she refused to talk to us. So we wrote to her, but she never responded to our letters." Allen let his shoulders slump. "We thought she just didn't want anything to do with us. So we left her alone. We should have tried harder, but there was so much animosity that it seemed somehow better just to let her go."

"Beth never mentioned getting any letters," Clay said, shaking his head.

Allen looked at Sara again. "That's because she never received them."

"How did that happen?" Clay asked.

"About three months ago we received a package from the people who bought Violet's house. It contained the unopened letters we had written to Beth. They found them in an old desk left in the basement when Beth moved."

Clay frowned. "Did Beth leave them there?"

"No, we believe Violet did. In the package was a letter she had written to Beth with an explanation, apology and a plea for forgiveness. She thought she'd withheld the letters so as not to let them upset Beth, but later she realized she wanted to keep Beth and little Maxwell close and not lose them to us. Apparently she wrote it just before she had her debilitating stroke and never had a chance to give it to Beth or even let her know our letters were there."

"That's so tragic," Clay replied.

"Yes, it was. Beth loved Violet and never would have abandoned her. She was so wonderful caring for her." Sara's voice cracked.

Clay nodded. "Beth told me how much her great-aunt meant to her."

"And Violet loved Beth and Maxwell. That's why she couldn't bear the thought of losing them. Because Violet never had a family of her own, Beth and her baby became that family. She was afraid if Beth read our letters, Violet would lose them. Her letter explained all that." Tears welled in Sara's eyes. "All those wasted years."

"So why didn't you try to find Beth after you received the package of letters?"

"We had no idea where she had gone. We found no

forwarding address. We didn't know where to start looking. And we couldn't afford to hire a private detective. All we could do was pray," Allen said.

"We inquired of some other relatives. We did searches on the Internet. Things we could afford. But none of those gave us any clues. It was as though she had vanished," Sara said tearfully.

"Did you ever think she wasn't trying to defy you, but that she really wanted her baby?" Clay asked.

Sadness deepened the lines across Allen's face as he nodded. "Now we do. We made so many mistakes. We've been praying that somehow we could find her."

"That's why I said you were an answer to our prayers," Sara added.

Clay shook his head. "I'm not the answer to your prayers. Having Beth turn her life back to God would be the answer to your prayers."

"You're right." Sara laid a hand on Clay's arm. "Do you think she will talk with us?"

"I'm hoping she will. If she talks with you, maybe there's hope for me, too."

"It's all your fault, Mom. Clay would've come back if it weren't for you. First you ignored his e-mails. Then you told him not to come for Thanksgiving. Now Christmas, too." Max glared as he stood in his bedroom doorway.

Beth wanted to cry. Even her own son was turning against her. Shaking her head, she tried to glare back. "No, Max. He wouldn't have come back. At least not to stay. His job takes him wherever. This time it's Seattle. The next time it could be Alaska, Florida, or New York."

"But if you'd asked him to stay, he would have!" Max shouted, slamming his palm against the doorjamb.

"That's what you think, but you don't know." Beth forced herself to speak calmly. She couldn't let Max know how much his accusations hurt.

"Why did you tell him to stay away?"

"You wouldn't understand. This is between Clay and me. It doesn't involve you."

"It sure does involve me. He's my friend, too. Just because you don't want him around doesn't mean I don't." Max stomped across the room. "Since you don't want him around for Christmas, maybe I'll just see about spending Christmas with him."

"And how do you propose to do that?"

"It's two weeks till Christmas. If I let him know I want to come, he'll send me the money for a plane ticket."

Beth wondered whether Clay would do that if Max asked. Surely Clay wouldn't betray her further. "Don't you understand how wrong it was for him not to tell me about what you had done?"

"He was just trying to help me. And he did. Doesn't that count for anything?"

Beth couldn't argue with Max, but that didn't make what Clay had done right. "It still doesn't change the fact that I'm your mother, and he should've told me."

"Why can't you forgive him? He thought he was doing the right thing."

"I have forgiven him, but that doesn't change the fact that he's got obligations elsewhere, and he's not coming back to stay." Why did Max have to argue about this? Having Clay come back temporarily would only prolong the hurt of his next good-bye, and Beth didn't want any man hurting her son by leaving anymore. A permanent break was the best thing for them all.

Max continued arguing. "You're just against anything that has to do with God. You complain that people didn't forgive you for your mistakes, but people here have gone out of their way to include us. Especially Clay. Why are you so against him? Why are you so against God?"

Beth pressed her lips together to keep them from quivering. She couldn't tell him the whole truth about her past. It would be too hurtful to him. So, no matter what he thought of her, she had to protect him.

"Max, I'm sorry I can't forget that even my own parents turned against me because of God."

"Maybe your parents have changed. Did you ever try to talk to them about me? Maybe they'd like me."

Max's question socked Beth in the gut. Was she hurting her son because she couldn't face the people who had hurt her? Was she letting her fears rob him of grandparents? No. She was saving him from their rejection. "Max, I've only been trying to protect you."

"Well, don't do me any more favors." Max's voice cracked.

She crossed the room and placed her hand on his arm. "I wish you'd understand."

He jerked away. "Just leave me alone. I'm going over to Brittany's. At least over there they know how to be a family." He shrugged into his jacket, grabbed his book bag and slung it over his shoulder. "I'm outta here."

"Maxwell Carlson!" Beth yelled after him.

Ignoring her, he raced out the door, not bothering to close it. He nearly knocked Kim off her feet as she climbed the front steps. He didn't stop but ran down the street.

With raised eyebrows, Kim stepped into the living room and went to Beth's side. "What's wrong?"

"Max hates me. Everyone hates me."

"Nobody hates you." Kim patted Beth on the back. "Would you like to tell me what happened?"

"I guess." Nodding, Beth sat on the couch.

Kim sat next to her. "Okay, tell me what's going on."

Beth leaned back and breathed deeply, trying to calm her mind. How could she tell Kim? Her friend would side with Max and Clay. They wanted to serve God. Could she be part of that? Could she forgive her parents and make things right with them? The gulf seemed so wide. How could she cross it? Closing her eyes for a moment, Beth drank in the quietness. The only sound came from the ticking of the clock. The ticking matched her heartbeat. Each tick reminded her of Clay. Each beat magnified the pain.

Finally she opened her eyes and looked at Kim. "Max is angry with me because I didn't want to invite Clay for Thanksgiving or Christmas." Beth told Kim about Max's being grounded, Clay's unanswered e-mails and Max's accusations. Beth explained the whole sorry mess. When she finished, she bit her lower lip and closed her eyes to keep from crying.

Kim touched her arm. "Did you ever think Max might be right? You've been pushing God away ever since I met you. It seems to me when you've felt like you might give in to God's calling, you pushed away the people who could help."

Opening her eyes, Beth shook her head. "I didn't push you away."

"True, but you've always kept me at arm's length."

Beth didn't know what to say. She thought about her relationship with Kim. Beth had always been glad Kim never pried into her past, but was that keeping her at a distance?

Beth's heart sank further. She felt as though she was dying inside. "I haven't been a very good friend. I'm sorry."

"Beth, I've never felt that way. You're an excellent friend. You've simply kept me far enough away so that you didn't have to share too many details of your past with me."

Releasing a shaky breath, Beth nodded. "I was afraid if you knew about my past that you wouldn't accept me."

"What could be so bad about your past that I wouldn't accept you?"

Twisting her hands in her lap, Beth avoided Kim's gaze. "I just thought church people would look down on me because I wasn't married to Max's father. That's the way I was treated when I got pregnant."

"Beth, we're all sinners in need of God's grace."

"Clay said that, too."

"He's right. God can take even the things we do wrong and somehow make them work out for good. We just have to let Him into our lives. Let God's love fill us."

"Sometimes I want to believe that, but I'm so afraid." Beth pressed her lips together.

Kim took Beth's hands in hers. "Will you let me pray for you?"

Beth nodded.

Kim bowed her head, and Beth did the same.

"Father, you know Beth's heart. Help her in this time of distress with Max. Help her to let You back into her life so she can rely on You for the wisdom she needs in

raising her son. Please, Lord, help her to know how Your grace absolves our sins."

As Kim continued to pray, the tears that Beth had been holding back flooded her eyes and spilled onto her cheeks. Sobs racked her body.

While the tears ran down her face, Beth poured her heart out to God. *"Lord, thank You for sending Kim into my life so she could remind me that You love me even though I don't deserve it. Help me be a good mom to Max, and just help me. I need You."* Her sobs overwhelmed her. She couldn't say another word.

Holding Beth, Kim prayed until Beth's crying subsided, then reached into her purse and handed her a couple of tissues.

After she wiped her nose and face, Beth looked up at Kim. "Thank you."

Kim gave her another hug. "I've been praying for this day since I met you."

"I'm sure glad you didn't give up on me." Beth mustered a smile.

"God's the one who didn't give up on you." She paused. "You need to tell Clay about your decision. He would want to know."

Beth sighed. "I said some awful things to him before he left."

"He'll forgive you."

"I hope so."

"Well, what are you waiting for? Let's call him."

"I don't have his number. I could send an e-mail."

"Not e-mail," Kim said, shaking her head. "You have to talk with him. Does Max have his number?"

"Yes."

Kim grabbed Beth's arm. "Get your coat so we can find Max and get that number. He'll be thrilled about your decision."

Boarding the plane, Clay gripped his cell phone as he anxiously hoped for a call from Beth's parents, but none came. He had wanted to stay with them until they talked with Beth, but he had to leave in order to catch his plane back to Seattle. The time difference between Ohio and Washington forced them to wait to call until Beth would be home from school.

When Clay left, Allen and Sara had promised to call and give Clay a report as soon as they talked with Beth. They had also promised not to mention how they had found her. He didn't want her to know he was interfering in her life again. Time was running out for the Carlsons to call. Any minute now the flight attendant would announce that passengers must turn off their phones.

Clay's mind whirled with questions and possibilities. Maybe Beth had refused to talk to her parents. Maybe they had talked, and the conversation hadn't gone well. Should he call them to check? Waiting and worrying was giving him a headache.

In desperation he scrolled through his contact numbers. Just as he was about to place the call, the flight attendant made the announcement about cell phones. Now he would have to wait until his layover in Denver to receive any messages or calls. Slumping in his seat, he turned off his cell phone and realized he had forgotten to pray. He shook his head. Why was it so easy to forget about God and try to rely on oneself? *Lord, I put this into Your hands. Help me to depend on You.*

As the plane soared above the earth, Clay thought about one of his favorite verses from the Bible found in Isaiah 40:31: *...but those who hope in the Lord will renew their strength. They will soar on wings like eagles; they will run and not grow weary, they will walk and not be faint.*

Gazing out the window as the lights of Dayton grew smaller, Clay knew he had to keep faith that Beth would forgive her parents and turn back to God. That would be the best Christmas gift of all. Even though Beth had ignored his attempts at communication, he prayed that the Christmas spirit would soften her heart. He was going to Pinecrest for Christmas. The plan was set for him to stay in his old apartment, since Maria was going to be with her family in California over the holiday.

As soon as the plane touched down in Denver, Clay turned on his cell phone. Still no message from Beth's parents. He had to call them. He couldn't stand not knowing whether they had talked to her. His stomach churned as he called their number. After speaking with Allen, Clay just had more questions. Every time they had called, there was no answer. What were Beth and Max doing? They should've been home from school by now. Maybe they were Christmas shopping in Spokane?

As Clay slipped his phone into his pocket, it rang. His heart jumped into his throat. He looked at the display screen on the phone. The call came from the Gormans, not Beth's parents. Why were the Gormans calling?

He punched the button to answer the call. "Hello?"

"Clay?" Max's eager voice sounded in Clay's ear.

"Yeah, Max. What's happening?"

"The best thing ever. My mom has turned her life back to the Lord."

Clay nearly shouted hallelujah as he walked down the concourse toward his departure gate. "Praise God. That's wonderful news. Tell me about it."

"I'll let you talk to her."

"Sure." Clay's stomach churned as he waited to hear Beth's voice. Had she talked to her parents? Max hadn't mentioned them.

"Hi." Her shy greeting made his heart pound even faster.

"Hi. Max told me your good news. I'm so glad. When did you make this decision?"

"Tonight," she replied, and then she proceeded to tell him what had happened. "I finally realized I couldn't live without God. Thanks to you and Kim."

"Does this mean you've forgiven me?"

"Yes. Max wants you to come for Christmas."

"What about you? Do *you* want me to come?"

"Yes."

Her answer made his heart soar—until he remembered her parents. What about them? How did he ask without letting on he had seen them? "So you've been at the Gormans' house for a while?"

"Yeah. We prayed together. Then we ordered pizza and had a little celebration. We've actually been trying to call you for a couple of hours, but we kept getting your voice mail."

"I didn't have my phone on because I was on an airplane. Why didn't you leave a message?"

"Not the kind of thing I wanted to leave in a voice mail."

"I understand. I got your call as soon as I got off the plane, so I probably wouldn't have gotten a message any sooner anyway." Clay wanted so much to tell Beth that he loved her, but that was something better said in person. So he would wait until he was in Pinecrest for Christmas. "I have a very short layover, and they're already boarding. I won't be able to talk much longer. I'll call you tomorrow from Seattle."

"I'll be waiting."

Two weeks later Beth paced back and forth across the living-room floor. She stopped and gazed out the window at the Christmas lights twinkling on the bushes in the dusk. Then she turned to Max. "Do you suppose they ran into bad weather?"

"Mom, the weather's fine. They said they wouldn't be here until six o'clock." He glanced at his watch. "It's not even five-thirty."

"I know. Do you think the house looks okay?"

"Mom, it looks fine. I'm exhausted from helping you clean."

Beth went over and gave Max a hug. "You've been a huge help. I just want everything to be perfect."

"It's perfect. All Grandma and Grandpa want to do is see us, not check for dust."

"You're right," Beth said, trying not to burden Max with her problem of getting over critical voices from the past.

The thought of this meeting had her tied into knots. Since she had received the unexpected phone call from her folks two weeks ago, she had waited for Christmas Eve with excitement and apprehension. Although tearful apologies and heartfelt prayers and professions of forgiveness had permeated their phone conversations, how was she going to feel upon seeing her parents in person? Despite the words of reconciliation they had shared, could she really put the past behind her? Would it color her feelings, affect Max's relationship with his grandparents?

Beth looked at the Christmas tree, sparkling with lights and ornaments, some new and some old. The new ones were gifts from the kindergarten students. They symbolized her new beginning in Pinecrest. The old ones brought back pleasant memories of her great-aunt Violet.

"What are you thinking about, Mom?"

Beth turned and smiled, trying to cover up her nervousness. "I was just looking at the ornaments." She went over to the tree and touched a tiny silver star. "Do you remember this one?"

Max nodded. "Aunt Violet helped me make that. I still miss her."

"Me, too."

Max placed an arm around Beth's shoulders. "You're worried about seeing Grandma and Grandpa, aren't you?"

"How'd you guess?" She looked up at her son. "How did you get to be so smart and grown up?"

"I have a great mom."

"I'm glad you think so, but remember that next time we have a disagreement," she said, a lump forming in her throat.

"I'm going to give Brittany a call."

While she watched Max lope into the kitchen, she cherished their renewed closeness. Although he gave her all the credit for his maturity, Beth knew that his recent friendship with Clay had had a big influence on her adolescent son. And Clay's visit tomorrow would trigger another emotional avalanche. Was she ready to deal with that, too? Her renewal of faith resolved one issue that stood between them. But other problems remained. He didn't like small towns, and she was finally happy here in Pinecrest. She also found herself wondering what her parents would think of him.

Trying to put all troubling thoughts from her mind, she glanced at the Christmas tree again. This year for her, the tree, besides being a secular symbol of the holiday, brought with it all the spiritual hopes associated with Christmas and God's most wonderful gift of His Son. Her heart swelled with joy over the decision she had made to return to God. She had to remember to lean on His strength to deal with her parents and Clay.

Lord, thank You for helping me find my way. Please give my parents and Clay safety as they travel. May our reunions bring peace to our lives.

Beth released an audible sigh as she looked out the window again. A car pulled to the curb and stopped. Its lights went out. Her stomach clenched. "Max, they're here!" she called as her heart hammered. She felt glued to the floor. "Max?"

"I'm coming. I had to say good-bye to Brittany." He raced into the living room and stopped. "Well, what are we waiting for?" He grabbed her hand and dragged her to the front door and threw it open.

Cold December air swept into the house, but warmth flooded Beth's chest as her parents, carrying bags of brightly wrapped Christmas gifts, stepped onto the porch. In seconds the gifts sat on the porch, and Beth found herself engulfed in a tearful group hug just inside the doorway.

After they finally broke away from one another, Max

and her father carried the packages into the house and set them under the tree. Then they all started to talk at once. Laughter filled the air. Beth laughed and cried at the same time.

Sara pulled Beth into her embrace again. "Finding you is the best Christmas present I've ever had." Then Sara turned to Max. "And what a double blessing to have such a handsome grandson."

"Thanks. I'm glad to finally meet my grandparents." Max looked embarrassed but gave his grandmother another hug.

"You look wonderful." His voice husky, Beth's father hugged her. "And you have a lovely place here."

Beth basked in her father's compliments. She so wanted to please him, even after all the years of bitterness. Did her father seem smaller, or had he just appeared larger than life when she was a girl? Her parents had aged, no doubt about it. "Thanks, Dad. I have potato soup ready to eat. Just like Mom used to make on Christmas Eve."

"Before we eat, your mom and I need to freshen up a little." Her dad glanced around. "Where can we do that?"

"Max, show them where the bathroom is, and I'll set the table." Beth started toward the kitchen.

Her dad waylaid her by putting a hand on her arm. "Before you do that, I need you to go out to our car and bring in one more gift." He handed her the car keys. "It's in the back seat."

"Sure." She took the keys and headed out the door.

Despite her heavy sweater, she shivered in the cold air as she unlocked the car. When she opened the door, the dome light illuminated a figure in the back seat.

Then, through the fog of her confusion, she heard a familiar voice. Clay's voice.

"Beth, it's me." He reached out to her.

She shook her head in amazement. "What are you doing here? I thought you weren't coming until tomorrow. And what are you doing in my parents' car?"

"One question at a time." He pulled her into the car. "Close the door, and I'll answer them all."

Sitting in his embrace, Beth listened while Clay explained everything about his visit with his family and how he had decided to try to find her parents. "I didn't want to tell you because I didn't want you to be mad that I was interfering in your life again. But I couldn't keep it a secret from you any longer. I had to risk complete disclosure."

She smiled and leaned her head against his shoulder. "You can interfere in my life anytime you want from now on."

"That's good to know." He reached down and picked up a big box wrapped in gold paper and ribbons. He held it out to her. "Merry Christmas."

Sitting straighter, she took the present. "Shouldn't I wait until tomorrow?"

"In my family, we always opened one gift apiece on Christmas Eve. I want you to open this one."

"Okay." She ripped away the paper, and lilting musical notes sounded as she popped the box open. "A music box. I love it!"

Clay chuckled. "But you haven't even seen it yet."

"I don't have to see it. I know I'll love it." She threw her arms around his neck and held him close. "I've missed you."

Clay pulled out of her embrace and gazed into her eyes. "I've missed you, too." He took the box. "Let me help you get this out. You grab hold of the foam packing, and I'll pull on the box."

More music floated through the air as Beth lifted the music box from its packaging. When the packing fell away, Beth held an ornately carved carousel in her hands. She looked at Clay, and tears sprang to her eyes. "You remembered my favorite music box that got broken. Thank you," she blubbered. "I've got to quit crying or my eyes will be puffy."

"Can't have that." Clay brushed a tear from her cheek with his thumb. "If you'll look closer, one of the horses has something special hanging from its brass pole."

Squinting, Beth looked over the carousel until she saw something sparkling in the dim light from the street-lamps. A ring. A diamond ring. She forgot to breathe as she looked at Clay.

"Beth, I love you. Will you marry me? I don't want to be alone in the big city anymore. I want to be here in Pine-crest with you and Max. And I know we can make it work."

More tears welled in her eyes. "Oh, yes, I love you so much, but you're making me cry all over again."

"You're sure you can deal with the traveling I have to do in my job?"

She laughed through her tears. "Yes, because I know you'll come back to me."

"Always." He took the ring off the brass pole and placed it on her finger, then kissed her. When the kiss ended, he grabbed her hand. "Let's go show Max and your parents."

When they emerged from the car, Beth saw Max and

her parents peering out the window. Joy filled her heart as her family rushed into the yard to greet them. She burst out laughing. "You all knew."

Clay held her close. "Yeah. I had to ask your dad for your hand. And I needed Max's approval."

"Mom, I'm so happy for all of us. This makes it the best Christmas ever." Max gave her a hug and shook Clay's hand.

"Yes, the best Christmas ever." Beth smiled at Max.

"Congratulations," Beth's dad said, shaking Clay's hand and giving Beth a hug. "Now let's get out of the cold and have some of that soup."

"Thanks, Dad." As she held Clay's hand and scurried up the walk, something wet hit her nose. White flakes fell from the darkened sky.

Max took the front steps in one leap. "Cool, a white Christmas!"

While the others hurried into the house, Beth stopped for a moment and watched the beauty of the falling snow. She glanced at Clay, who pulled her into his arms and kissed her while the snow fell around them.

When the kiss ended, she walked hand in hand with Clay onto the porch. Just before she went into the house, Beth looked heavenward and whispered, "Thank You, Lord, for the gift of love."

* * * * *

Dear Reader,

Thank you for choosing to read *Love Walked In*.
I enjoyed writing this story because it gave me the
opportunity to revisit my imaginary town of Pinecrest,
Washington, and peek in on the characters from
The Heart's Homecoming, my first book with
Steeple Hill. The area around Spokane, Washington,
is a place familiar to me as I lived there during my
high school years. It is a region of wonderful natural
beauty that truly shows God's handiwork.

I loved giving Max's mom from *The Heart's Homecoming*
a name and her own story as she learns to cope with
a teenage son while finding God's grace and love. In
writing this story, I wanted to share the wonder of God's
grace and His ever-present love demonstrated by the gift
of Jesus. I hope something from Beth and Clay's story
will touch your heart.

I love hearing from readers. You can contact me at
P.O. Box 16461, Fernandina Beach, FL 32035, or
through my Web site www.merrilleewhren.com.

May God bless you.

Merrillee Whren

QUESTIONS FOR DISCUSSION

1. Because of Beth's past experience, when she first meets Clay, she makes some judgments about him based on his appearance and mode of transportation. Have you ever judged someone by how they look? How does God judge a person? What does the Bible say about judging others?

2. Kim and Clay want Beth to turn her life back to God. What methods do they employ to bring Beth back to the Lord? Do you think this is an effective plan? How can Christians influence the people in their lives? Consider 1 John 3:17 in your discussion.

3. Clay warns Beth about one of Max's friends. What prompted this warning? What can parents do to make sure their children have friends that won't lead them in the wrong direction? What light do Proverbs 22:6 and Ephesians 6:4 shed on this subject?

4. Clay confronts Max about his underage drinking, but doesn't tell Beth. Do you think Clay did the right thing in not telling her? How would you handle a situation such as this? How can parents and other adults influence kids not to drink or bow to peer pressure?

5. Beth worries about how the church folks will view her. She feels they will judge her unkindly. Have you ever known someone who thought they couldn't live up to the expectations of others? How can Christians share the gospel and show people that they can come to the Lord without being perfect?

6. Beth is nervous about Max's participation in football, but she still allows him to be on the team. Do you think it is important for parents to support the activities in which their children are involved? What perspective should a Christian apply to such a situation? How can a parent encourage their children to choose activities that will help them grow as individuals?

7. Why is Clay concerned about his attraction to Beth? How does he deal with it? Do you think he handled it in the correct way? Have you or someone you know been in a similar situation? How did you or the other person deal with it?

8. A crisis in Beth's life finally makes her realize she needs to rely on God. Has a crisis in your life ever brought you closer to God? How did your relationship with God help you with your problem?

9. Beth says that her father preached the rules. Clay tells her that Christianity is about the grace of God. Why is it important to remember God's grace?

10. Clay believes it is important for Beth to reconcile with God and her parents. Have you or someone you know been estranged from a family member? How can faith in God bring a person to reconcile with someone who has hurt them? What does 1 John 4:20 say about this?

REQUEST YOUR FREE BOOKS!

2 FREE INSPIRATIONAL NOVELS
PLUS 2
FREE
MYSTERY GIFTS

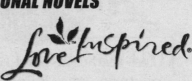

YES! Please send me 2 FREE Love Inspired® novels and my 2 FREE mystery gifts. After receiving them, if I don't wish to receive any more books, I can return the shipping statement marked "cancel." If I don't cancel, I will receive 4 brand-new novels every month and be billed just $3.99 per book in the U.S., or $4.74 per book in Canada, plus 25¢ shipping and handling per book and applicable taxes, if any*. That's a savings of at least 20% off the cover price! I understand that accepting the 2 free books and gifts places me under no obligation to buy anything. I can always return a shipment and cancel at any time. Even if I never buy another book from Steeple Hill, the two free books and gifts are mine to keep forever.

113 IDN EF26   313 IDN EF27

Name	(PLEASE PRINT)	
Address		Apt.
City	State/Prov.	Zip/Postal Code
Signature (if under 18, a parent or guardian must sign)		

Order online at www.LoveInspiredBooks.com

Or mail to Steeple Hill Reader Service™:

IN U.S.A.	IN CANADA
P.O. Box 1867	P.O. Box 609
Buffalo, NY	Fort Erie, Ontario
14240-1867	L2A 5X3

Not valid to current Love Inspired subscribers.

Want to try two free books from another series?
Call 1-800-873-8635 or visit www.morefreebooks.com

* Terms and prices subject to change without notice. NY residents add applicable sales tax. Canadian residents will be charged applicable provincial taxes and GST. This offer is limited to one order per household. All orders subject to approval. Credit or debit balances in a customer's account(s) may be offset by any other outstanding balance owed by or to the customer. Please allow 4 to 6 weeks for delivery.

LIREG06

TITLES AVAILABLE NEXT MONTH

Don't miss these four stories in January

RAINBOW'S END by Irene Hannon

When a storm stranded widower Keith Michaels on Orcas Island, he sought refuge with young widow Jill Whelan. She gave Keith hope that the road to faith and love could lead to Rainbow's End.

HEARTS AFIRE by Marta Perry
The Flanagans

For firefighter paramedic Terry Flanagan, her clinic for migrant workers was a way to make a difference. But when handsome Dr. Jacob Landsdowne was assigned to oversee her project, she wondered if her dreams would go up in smoke.

WHEN LOVE COMES HOME by Arlene James

Paige Ellis's kidnapped son had finally come home. But her little boy was now a surly teen. She turned to her attorney Grady Jones for help. Grady was clueless about women, yet Paige made him contemplate making her family his own.

A HUSBAND FOR ALL SEASONS by Irene Brand

Though an accident cut Chad Reece's football career short, he was determined to recover on his own. But then he met hospital volunteer Vicky Lanham. Her passion for helping others made Chad want to join with her in her mission and her life.